SLAVE

(OF CR

MORGAN RICE

To Storm Jensen,
a remarkable wife, mother, and hero.
Every word is a step—and you, Storm, are brave enough to start.

"Come close, dear warrior, and I shall tell you a tale.
A tale of battles distant.
A tale of men and valor.
A tale of crowns and glory."

--The Forgotten Chronicles of Lysa

CHAPTER ONE

Ceres ran through the back alleys of Delos, excitement coursing through her veins, knowing she could not be late. The sun was barely rising, and yet the muggy, dust-filled air was already suffocating in the ancient stone city. Legs burning, lungs aching, she nonetheless pushed herself to run faster, and faster still, hopping over one of the countless rats that crept out of the gutters and refuse in the streets. She could already hear the distant rumble, and her heart pounded with anticipation. Somewhere ahead, she knew, the Festival of the Killings was about to begin.

Letting her hands drag along the stone walls as she twisted and turned down a narrow alley, Ceres glanced back to make certain her brothers were keeping up. There, she was relieved to see, were Nesos, at her heels, and Sartes, only a few feet behind. At nineteen, Nesos was just two sun cycles older than she, while Sartes, her baby brother, four sun cycles younger, was on the verge of manhood. The two of them, with their longish sandy hair and brown eyes, looked exactly like each other—and their parents—and yet nothing like her. Still, though Ceres might be a girl, they had never been able to keep pace with her.

"Hurry!" Ceres yelled over her shoulder.

Another rumble came, and although she had never been to the festival, she imagined it in vivid detail: the entire city, all three million citizens of Delos, crowding into the Stade on this summer solstice holiday. It would be unlike anything she had seen before, and if her brothers and she didn't hurry, not a single seat would remain.

Picking up speed, Ceres wiped a drop of sweat off her brow and smeared it onto her frayed, ivory tunic, a hand-me-down from her mother. She had never been given new clothes. According to her mother, who doted on her brothers but seemed to reserve a special hatred and envy for her, she didn't deserve it.

"Wait!" Sartes yelled, an edge of irritation in his cracking voice.

Ceres smiled.

"Shall I carry you, then?" she yelled back.

She knew that he hated it when she teased him, yet her snide remark would motivate him to keep up. Ceres didn't mind his tagging along; she thought it was endearing how he, at thirteen, would do anything to be considered their peer. And even though she would never admit it openly, a huge part of her needed him to need her.

1

Sartes gave a loud grunt.

"Mother will kill you when she finds out you disobeyed her again!" he yelled back.

He was right. Indeed, she would—or give her a good flogging, at least.

The first time her mother had beaten her, at the age of five, it was the very moment Ceres lost her innocence. Before then, the world had been fun, kind, and good. After that, nothing had ever been safe again, and all that she had to hold onto was her hope of a future where she could get away from her. She was older now, close, and yet even that dream was slowly eroding in her heart.

Fortunately, Ceres knew her brothers would never tell on her. They were as loyal to her as she was to them.

"Then it's a good thing Mother will never know!" she cried back.

"Father will find out, though!" Sartes snapped.

She chuckled. Father already knew. They had made a deal: if she stayed up late to finish sharpening the swords due for delivery at the palace, she could go see the Killings. And so she did.

Ceres reached the wall at the end of the lane and, without pausing, wedged her fingers in two cracks and began to climb. Her hands and feet moved swiftly, and up she went, a good twenty feet, until she scrambled to the top.

She stood, breathing hard, and the sun greeted her with its bright rays. She shaded her eyes with a hand.

She gasped. Normally, the Old City was dotted with a few citizens, a stray cat or dog here and there—yet today it was positively alive. It swarmed with people. Ceres could not even see the cobblestones beneath the sea of people pressing into Fountain Square.

In the distance the ocean shimmered a vivid blue, while the towering white Stade stood as a mountain amongst twisting roads and sardine-packed two- and three-story houses. Around the outer edge of the plaza merchants had lined up booths, each eager to sell food, jewelry, or clothes.

A gust of wind brushed against her face, and the smell of freshly baked goods seeped into her nostrils. What she wouldn't give for food that would satisfy that gnawing sensation. She wrapped her arms around her belly as she felt a hunger pang. Breakfast this morning had been a few spoonfuls of soggy porridge, which had somehow managed to leave her stomach feeling hungrier than before she ate it. Given that today was her eighteenth birthday, she had hoped for at least a little extra food in her bowl—or a hug or *something*.

But no one had mentioned a word. She doubted they even remembered.

Light caught her eyes, and Ceres looked down to spot a golden carriage weaving through the crowd like a bubble through honey, slow and shiny. She frowned. In her excitement, she had failed to consider that the royalty would be at the event, too. She despised them, their haughtiness, that their animals were better fed than most of the people of Delos. Her brothers were hopeful that one day, they would triumph over the class system. But Ceres did not share their optimism: if there were to be any sort of equality in the Empire, it would have to come by way of revolution.

"Do you see him?" Nesos panted as he climbed up beside her.

Ceres's heart quickened as she thought of him. Rexus. She, too, had been wondering if he was here yet, and had been scanning the crowds to no avail.

She shook her head.

"There." Nesos pointed.

She followed his finger toward the fountain, squinting.

Suddenly she saw him, and could not suppress her burst of excitement. It was the same way she always felt when she saw him. There he was, sitting on the edge of the fountain, tightening his bow. Even from this distance, she could see his shoulder and chest muscles move beneath his tunic. Hardly a few years older than she, he had blond hair that stood out amongst heads of black and brown, and his tan skin glistened in the sun.

"Wait!" cried a voice.

Ceres glanced back down the wall to see Sartes, struggling with the climb.

"Hurry up or we'll leave you behind!" Nesos goaded.

Of course, they wouldn't dream of leaving their younger brother, although he did need to learn to keep up. In Delos, a moment of weakness could mean death.

Nesos ran a hand through his hair, catching his breath, too, as he surveyed the crowd.

"So who is your money on to win?" he asked.

Ceres turned to him and laughed.

"What money?" she asked.

He smiled.

"If you had any," he answered.

"Brennius," she replied without pausing.

His brow lifted in surprise.

3

"Really?" he asked. "Why?"

"I don't know." She shrugged. "Just a hunch."

But she did know. She knew very well, better than her brothers, better than all the boys of her city. Ceres had a secret: she hadn't told anyone she had, on occasion, dressed as a boy and trained at the palace. It was forbidden by royal decree for girls—punishable by death—to learn the ways of the combatlords, yet male commoners were welcome to learn in exchange for equal amounts of work in the palace's stables, work which she did happily.

She'd watched Brennius and had been impressed by the way he fought. He wasn't the largest of the combatlords, yet his moves were calculated with precision.

"No chance," Nesos replied. "It'll be Stefanus."

She shook her head.

"Stefanus will be dead within the first ten minutes," she said flatly.

Stefanus was the obvious choice, the largest of the combatlords, and probably the strongest; yet he wasn't as calculating as Brennius or some of the other warriors she had watched.

Nesos barked a laugh.

"I'll give you my good sword if that's the case."

She glanced at the sword attached to his waist. He had no idea how jealous she had been when he received that masterpiece of a weapon as a birthday gift from Mother three years ago. Her sword was an old leftover one her father had tossed into the recycling pile. Oh, the things she'd be able to do if she had a weapon like Nesos's.

"I'm going to hold you to it, you know," Ceres said, smiling— although in reality, she would never take his sword from him.

"I'd expect nothing less," he smirked.

She crossed her arms in front of her chest as a dark thought crossed her mind.

"Mother wouldn't allow it," she said.

"But Father would," he said. "He's very proud of you, you know."

Nesos's kind comment took her off guard, and not knowing exactly how to accept it, she lowered her eyes. She loved her father dearly, and he loved her, she knew. Yet for some reason, her mother's face appeared before her. All she ever wanted was for her mother to accept her and love her as much as her brothers. But as hard as she tried, Ceres felt she could never be enough in her eyes.

Sartes grunted as he climbed the last step behind them. He was still about a head shorter than Ceres and as scrawny as a cricket, but she was convinced he'd sprout like a bamboo shoot any day now.

That's what had happened to Nesos. Now he was a muscle-bound hunk, hovering at six foot three.

"And you?" Ceres turned to Sartes. "Who do you think will win?"

"I'm with you. Brennius."

She smiled and ruffled his hair. He always said whatever she said.

Another rumble came, the crowd thickened, and she felt the urgency.

"Let's go," she said, "no time to waste."

Without waiting, Ceres climbed down the wall and hit the ground running. Keeping the fountain in sight, she made her way across the plaza, eager to reach Rexus.

He turned and his eyes widened in delight as she neared. She rushed into him and felt his arms wrap around her waist, as he pressed a scruffy cheek against hers.

"Ciri," he said in his low, raspy voice.

A shiver ran through her spine as she spun around to meet Rexus's cobalt blue eyes. At six foot one, he was nearly a head taller than her, and blond, coarse hair framed his heart-shaped face. He smelled like soap and the outdoors. Heavens, it was good to see him again. Even though she could fend for herself in nearly any situation, his presence brought her a sense of calm.

Ceres raised herself up onto the balls of her feet and curled willing arms around his thick neck. She had never seen him as more than a friend until she heard him speak of the revolution, and of the underground army he was a member of. "We will fight to free ourselves from the yoke of oppression," he had said to her years ago. He had spoken with such passion about the rebellion that for a moment, she had really believed overthrowing the royals was possible.

"How was the hunt?" she asked with a smile, knowing he had been gone for days.

"I missed your smile." He stroked her long, rose-gold hair back. "And your emerald eyes."

Ceres had missed him, too, but she didn't dare say. She was too afraid to lose the friendship they had if anything were to happen between them.

"Rexus," Nesos said, catching up, Sartes at his heels, and clasping his arm.

"Nesos," he said, in his deep, authoritative voice. "We have little time if we are to get in," he added, nodding to the others.

They all hurried off, merging with the throng heading toward the Stade. Empire soldiers were everywhere, urging the crowds forward, sometimes with clubs and whips. The closer they came to the road that led to the Stade, the more the crowd thickened.

All of a sudden, Ceres heard a clamor by one of the booths and she instinctively turned toward the sound. She saw that a generous space had opened up around a small boy, flanked by two Empire soldiers and a merchant. A few onlookers fled, while others gawked in a circle.

Ceres rushed forward to see one of the soldiers slap an apple out of the boy's hand as he grabbed the little one's arm, shaking him violently.

"Thief!" the soldier growled.

"Mercy, please!" the boy screamed, tears streaming down his dirty, hollow cheeks. "I was…so hungry!"

Ceres felt her heart burst from compassion, as she had felt the same hunger—and she knew the soldiers would be nothing short of cruel.

"Let the boy go," the heavyset merchant said calmly with the gesture of a hand, his gold ring catching the sunlight. "I can afford to give him an apple. I have hundreds of apples." He chuckled a little, as if to make light of the situation.

But the crowd gathered around and quieted as the soldiers turned to confront the merchant, their shiny armor rattling. Ceres's heart dropped for the merchant—she knew that one never risked confronting the Empire.

The soldier stepped forward menacingly toward the merchant.

"You defend a criminal?"

The merchant looked back and forth between the two of them, now seeming unsure. The soldier then turned and hit the boy across the face with a sickening crack that made Ceres shiver.

The boy fell to the ground with a thump as the crowd gasped.

Pointing at the merchant, the soldier said, "To prove your loyalty to the Empire, you will hold the boy while we flog him."

The merchant's eyes turned hard, his brow sweaty. To Ceres's surprise, he held his ground.

"No," he replied.

The second soldier took two threatening steps toward the merchant and his hand moved to the hilt of his sword.

"Do it, or you lose your head and we burn your shop down," the soldier said.

The merchant's round face went limp, and Ceres could tell he was defeated.

He slowly walked over to the boy and grabbed the boy's arms, kneeling in front of him.

"Please forgive me," he said, tears brimming in his eyes.

The boy whimpered and then started to scream as he tried to wring himself free from his grip.

Ceres could see the child was shaking. She wanted to keep moving toward the Stade, to avoid witnessing this, but instead, her feet stood frozen in the middle of the square, eyes glued to the brutality.

The first soldier tore the boy's tunic open while the second soldier whirled a flogger above his head. Most onlookers cheered the soldiers on, although a few murmured and walked away with heads hung low.

None defended the thief.

With a greedy, almost maddening expression, the soldier thrashed the whip against the boy's back, causing him to shriek in pain as they flogged him. Blood oozed out of the fresh lacerations. Again and again, the soldier flogged until the boy's head was sagging backward and he no longer screamed.

Ceres felt the strong urge to rush forward and save the boy. Yet to do so, she knew, would mean her death, and the death of all those she loved. She slumped her shoulders, feeling hopeless and defeated. Inwardly, she resolved to take revenge one day.

She yanked Sartes toward her and covered his eyes, desperately wanting to protect him, to give him a few more years of innocence, even though there was no innocence to be had in this land. She forced herself not to act on her impulse. As a man, he needed to see these instances of cruelty, not only to adapt, but also to one day be a strong contender in the rebellion.

The soldiers grabbed the boy out of the merchant's hands and then tossed his lifeless body into the back of a wooden cart. The merchant pressed his hands to his face and sobbed.

Within seconds, the cart was on its way, and the previously open space was again filled with people meandering about the square as if nothing had happened.

Ceres felt an overwhelming sense of nausea well up inside. It was unjust. In this moment, she could pick out a half a dozen pickpockets—men and women who had perfected their art so well that not even the Empire soldiers could catch them. This poor boy's life was now ruined because of his lack of skill. If caught, thieves, young or old, would lose their limbs or more, depending on how the judges felt that day. If he were lucky, his life would be spared and he would be sentenced to work in the gold mines for life. Ceres would rather die than have to endure being imprisoned like that.

They continued along the street, their mood ruined, shoulder to shoulder with the others as the heat grew almost unbearable.

A golden carriage pulled up next to them, forcing everyone out of the way, shoving people up to the houses on the sides. Jostled roughly, Ceres looked up to see three teenage girls in colorful silk dresses, pins of gold and precious jewels adorning their intricate up-dos. One of the teenagers, laughing, tossed a coin out onto the street, and a handful of commoners stooped onto hands and knees, scrambling for a piece of metal that would feed a family for an entire month.

Ceres never stooped to pick up any handouts. She'd rather starve than take donations from the likes of those.

She watched a young man get hold of the coin and an older man drive him to the ground and clamp a stiff hand around his neck. With the other hand, the older man forced the coin out of the young man's hand.

The teenage girls laughed and pointed fingers before their carriage continued to weave through the masses.

Ceres's insides clenched with disgust.

"In the near future, inequality will vanish forever," Rexus said. "I will see to it."

Listening to him speak, Ceres's chest swelled. One day she would fight side by side with him and her brothers in the rebellion.

As they neared the Stade the streets widened, and Ceres felt like she could take a breath. The air buzzed. She felt she would rupture from excitement.

She walked through one of the dozens of arched entrances and looked up.

Thousands upon thousands of commoners teemed inside the magnificent Stade. The oval structure had collapsed on the top northern side, and the majority of the red awnings were torn and provided little protection from the sweltering sun. Wild beasts growled from behind iron gates and trap doors, and she could see the combatlords standing ready behind the gates.

Ceres gaped, taking it all in in wonder.

Before she knew it, Ceres looked up and realized she had fallen behind Rexus and her brothers. She rushed forward to catch up, yet as soon as she did, four burly men had surrounded her. She smelled alcohol, rotting fish, and body odor as they pressed in too close, turning and gaping at her with rotted teeth and ugly smiles.

"You're coming with us, pretty girl," one of them said as they all strategically moved in on her.

Ceres heart raced. She looked ahead for the others, but they were already lost in the thickening crowd.

She confronted the men, trying to put on her bravest face.

"Leave me be or I will…"

They burst into laughter.

"What?" one mocked. "A wee girl like you take us four?"

"We could carry you out of here kickin' and screamin' and not a soul would say nuttin'," another added.

And it was true. From the corner of her eye, Ceres watched people rush by, pretending not to notice how these men were threatening her.

Suddenly, the leader's face turned serious, and with one swift move, he grabbed her arms and pulled her close. She knew they could haul her away, never to be seen again, and that thought terrified her more than anything.

Trying to ignore her pounding heart, Ceres spun around, snatching her arm out of his stronghold. The other men hooted in amusement, but when she thrust the base of her palm into the leader's nose, snapping his head back, they went silent.

The leader placed filthy hands over his nose and grunted.

She didn't relent. Knowing she had one chance, she kicked him once in the stomach, remembering her days of sparring, and he keeled over as she connected.

Immediately, though, the other three were upon her, their strong hands grabbing her, yanking her away.

Suddenly, they relented. Ceres looked over with relief to see Rexus appear and punch one in the face, knocking him out.

Nesos then appeared and grabbed another and kneed him in the stomach before kicking him to the ground, leaving him in the red dirt.

The fourth man charged toward Ceres, but just as he was about to attack, she ducked, spun, and kicked him in the rear so he went flying into a pillar headfirst.

She stood there, breathing hard, taking it all in.

Rexus placed a hand on Ceres's shoulder. "Are you all right?"

Ceres's heart was still running wild, but a feeling of pride slowly replaced her fear. She had done well.

She nodded and Rexus wrapped an arm around her shoulders as they continued on, his full lips gliding into a smile.

"What?" Ceres asked.

"When I saw what was happening, I wanted to run my sword through each and every one of them. But then I saw how you defended yourself." He shook his head and chuckled. "They didn't expect that."

She felt her cheeks flush. She wanted to say she had been fearless, but the truth was, she had not been.

"I was nervous," she admitted.

"Ciri, nervous? Never." He kissed Ceres on top of the head, and they continued into the Stade.

They found a few spots left at ground level and they took their seats, Ceres thrilled it was not too late as she put all the events of the day behind her and allowed herself to become caught up in the excitement of the cheering crowd.

"Do you see them?"

Ceres followed Rexus's finger and looked up to see a dozen or so teenagers sitting in a booth, sipping wine from silver goblets. She had never seen such fine clothing, so much food on one table, so much sparkling jewelry in her entire life. Not one of them had sunken cheeks or concave bellies.

"What are they doing?" she asked when she saw one of them collecting coins into a gold bowl.

"Each owns a combatlord," Rexus said, "and they place bets on who will win."

Ceres scoffed. This was just a game for them, she realized. Obviously, the spoiled teenagers didn't care about the warriors or about the art of combat. They just wanted to see if their combatlord would win. To Ceres, though, this event was about honor and courage and skill.

The royal banners were raised, trumpets blared, and as iron gates sprung open, one on each end of the Stade, combatlord after combatlord marched out of the black holes, their leather and iron armor catching the sunlight, emitting sparks of light.

The crowd roared as the brutes marched into the arena, and Ceres rose to her feet with them, applauding. The warriors ended in an outward-facing circle, their axes, swords, spears, shields, tridents, whips, and other weapons held to the sky.

"Hail, King Claudius," they yelled.

Trumpets blared again, and the golden chariot of King Claudius and Queen Athena whirled onto the arena from one of the entrances. Next, a chariot with Crown Prince Avilius, and Princess Floriana followed, and after them, an entire entourage of chariots carrying royals flooded the arena. Each chariot was towed by two snow white horses adorned with precious jewels and gold.

When Ceres spotted Prince Thanos amongst them, she became appalled at the nineteen-year-old boy's scowl. From time to time when she delivered swords for her father, she had seen him speak with the combatlords at the palace, and he always carried that sour expression of superiority. His physique lacked nothing when it came to the likes of a warrior—he could almost be mistaken for one—his arms bulging with muscle, his waist tight and muscular, and his legs hard as tree trunks. However, it infuriated her how he appeared to hold no respect or passion for his position.

As the royals paraded up to their places at the podium, trumpets blared again, signaling the Killings were about to begin.

The crowd roared as all but two combatlords vanished back into the iron gates.

Ceres recognized one of them as Stefanus, but she couldn't make out the other brute wearing nothing but a visored helmet and a loincloth secured by a leather belt. Perhaps he had traveled from afar to contend. His well-oiled skin was the color of fertile soil, and his hair as black as the darkest night. Through the slits in the helmet, Ceres could see the look of resolve in his eyes, and she knew in an instant that Stefanus wouldn't live to see another hour.

"Don't worry," Ceres said, glancing over at Nesos. "I'll let you keep your sword."

"He's not defeated yet," Nesos replied with a smirk. "Stefanus would not be everyone's favorite if he weren't superior."

When Stefanus lifted his trident and shield, the crowd went silent.

"Stefanus!" one of the wealthy male youths from the booth shouted with a raised clenched fist. "Power and bravery!"

Stefanus nodded toward the youth as the audience roared with approval, and then he came at the foreigner with full force. The foreigner swerved out of the way in a flash, spun around, and slashed at Stefanus with his sword, missing by a mere inch.

Ceres cringed. With reflexes like that, Stefanus wouldn't last long.

Hacking away at Stefanus's shield again and again, the foreigner roared while Stefanus retreated. Stefanus, desperate, finally flung the edge of his shield into his opponent's face, sending a spray of blood across the air as his foe fell.

Ceres thought that was a rather nice move. Maybe Stefanus had improved in his technique since she saw him in training last.

"Stefanus! Stefanus! Stefanus!" the spectators chanted.

Stefanus stood at the feet of the injured warrior, but just as he was about to stab him with the trident, the foreigner lifted his legs and kicked Stefanus so he tumbled backwards, landing on his behind. Both hopped to their feet as quick as cats and faced each other again.

Their eyes locked and they began circling one another, the danger in the air palpable, Ceres thought.

The foreigner snarled and lifted his sword high into the air as he ran toward Stefanus. Stefanus quickly veered to the side and jabbed him in the thigh. In return, the foreigner swung his sword around and sliced Stefanus's arm.

Both warriors grunted in pain, but it was as if the wounds drove their fury instead of slowing them. The foreigner peeled off his helmet and flung it to the ground. His black bearded chin was bloodied, his right eye swollen, but his expression made Ceres think he was done playing games with Stefanus and was going in for the kill. How quickly would he be able to slay him?

Stefanus charged toward the foreigner, and Ceres gasped as Stefanus's trident collided with his opponent's sword. Eyeball to eyeball the warriors strained against each other, grunting, panting, shoving, the blood vessels in their foreheads protruding and the muscles bulging beneath their sweaty skin.

The foreigner ducked and wringed out of the deadlock, and unexpected to Ceres, he spun around like a tornado, sliced through the air with his sword, and decapitated Stefanus.

After a few breaths, the foreigner triumphantly lifted his arm into the air.

For a second, the crowd went completely silent. Even Ceres. She glanced up at the teenage boy who was Stefanus's owner. His mouth was wide open, his eyebrows knit together in fury.

The teenage boy hurled his silver goblet into the arena and stormed out of the booth. Death is the great equalizer, Ceres thought as she suppressed a smile.

"August!" a man in the crowd yelled. "August! August!"

One after another the spectators joined in, until the entire stadium chanted the victor's name. The foreigner bowed to King Claudius, and then three other warriors came running from the iron gates, replacing him.

One fight after another ensued as the day grew long, and Ceres watched with eyes peeled. She couldn't quite make up her mind whether she hated the Killings or loved it. On one hand, she enjoyed watching the strategy, the skill, and the bravery of the contenders; yet on the other, she despised how the warriors were nothing but pawns to the wealthy.

As the last fight of the first round arrived, Brennius and another warrior fought right next to where Ceres, Rexus, and her brothers were sitting. Closer and closer they came, their swords clanking, sparks flying. It was thrilling.

Ceres watched as Sartes leaned over the railing, his eyes glued to the combatants.

"Lean back!" she yelled at him.

But before he could respond, all of a sudden, an omnicat jumped out from a hatch in the ground on the other side of the stadium. The huge beast licked its fangs and its claws dug into the red dirt as it made its way toward the warriors. The combatlords hadn't yet seen the animal, and the stadium held its breath.

"Brennius is dead," Nesos mumbled.

"Sartes!" Ceres yelled again. "I said get back—"

She didn't have a chance to finish her words. Just then, the rock beneath Sartes's hands loosened, and before anyone could react, he tumbled down, over the rail, and fell all the way into the pit, landing with a thud.

"Sartes!" Ceres yelled in horror as she shot to her feet.

Ceres looked down to see Sartes, ten feet below, sit up and lean his back against the wall. His lower lip quivered, but there were no tears. No words. Holding his arm, he looked upward, his face twisted in agony.

Seeing him down there was more than Ceres could bear. Without thinking, she drew Nesos's sword and leapt over the rail, hopping into the pit, landing right in front of her younger brother.

"Ceres!" Rexus yelled.

She glanced back up and saw guards hauling Rexus and Nesos away before they could follow.

Ceres stood in the pit, overcome with a surreal feeling to be down here with the fighters in the arena. She wanted to get Sartes out of there, but there was no time. So she stepped in front of him, determined to protect him as the omnicat roared at her. It hunched low, its wicked yellow eyes fixed on Ceres, and she could sense the danger.

She whipped Nesos's sword up with both hands and clenched it tight.

"Run, girl!" Brennius yelled.

But it was too late. Charging toward her, the omnicat was now only a few feet away. She stepped closer to Sartes and just before the animal attacked, Brennius came in from the side and sliced the beast's ear off.

The omnicat rose onto its hind legs and roared, clawing a chunk out of the wall behind Ceres as purple blood stained its fur.

The crowd roared.

The second combatlord approached, but before he could cause the beast any harm, the omnicat lifted its paw and slit the man's throat with its claws. Clamping his hands around his neck, the warrior collapsed to the ground, blood seeping through his fingers.

Hungry for blood, the crowd cheered.

Snarling, the omnicat hit Ceres so hard she went flying into the air, crashing to the ground. On impact, the sword went tumbling from her hand and landed several feet away.

Ceres lay there, her lungs refusing to open up. Dying for air, her head spinning, she tried to crawl up onto hands and knees, but quickly tumbled back down.

Lying breathless with her face pressed against the coarse sand, she saw the omnicat heading toward Sartes. Seeing her brother in such a defenseless state, she felt her insides ignite with fire. She forced herself to take a breath and she discerned with complete clarity what she needed to do to save her brother.

Energy rushed through her like a flood, giving her instant power, and she rose to her feet, picked up the sword, and dashed toward the beast so fast she was convinced she was flying.

The beast was ten feet away from her now. Eight. Six. Four.

Ceres gritted her teeth and flung herself onto the beast's back, digging insistent fingers into its bristly fur, desperate to distract it from her brother.

The omnicat stood up on hind legs and shook its upper body, jostling Ceres back and forth. But her iron grip and her resolve were stronger than the animal's attempts to throw her off.

As the creature lowered back onto all fours again, Ceres seized the opportunity. She raised her sword high into the air and stabbed the beast in the neck.

The animal screeched and rose onto hind legs, as the crowd roared.

Reaching a paw around to Ceres, the creature pierced her back with its claws, and Ceres screamed from the pain, the claws feeling like daggers through her flesh. The omnicat grabbed her and hurled her into the wall, and she landed several feet away from Sartes.

"Ceres!" Sartes yelled.

Ears ringing, Ceres struggled to sit up, the back of her head throbbing, warm liquid running down her neck. There was no time to assess how serious the wound was. The omnicat was charging her again.

As the beast bore down, Ceres was out of options. Not even thinking, she instinctively raised a palm and held it out before her. It was the last thing she thought she'd ever see.

Just as the omnicat pounced, Ceres felt as if a ball of fire ignited in her chest, and suddenly she felt a ball of energy shoot out of her hand.

Mid-air, the beast suddenly went limp.

It crashed to the ground, skidding to a halt on top of her legs. Half-expecting the animal to come to life again and finish her off, Ceres held her breath as she watched it lie there.

But the creature didn't move.

Baffled, Ceres glanced at her palm. Not having seen what transpired, the crowd probably thought the beast died because she had stabbed him with her sword earlier. But she knew better. Some mysterious force had left her hand and had killed the beast in an instant. What force was it? Never had anything like this occurred before, and she didn't quite know what to make of it.

Who was she to have this power?

Afraid, she let her hand fall to the earth.

She lifted hesitant eyes, and saw the stadium had gone silent.

And she could not help but wonder. Had they seen it, too?

CHAPTER TWO

For a second that seemed to stretch on and on, Ceres felt every eye upon her as she sat there, numb with pain and disbelief. More so than the repercussions to come, she feared the supernatural power that lurked within her, that had killed the omnicat. More than all the people surrounding her, she feared to face herself—a self she no longer knew.

Suddenly, the crowd, stunned into silence, roared. It took her a moment to realize that they were cheering for her.

A voice cut through the roars.

"Ceres!" Sartes yelled, beside her. "Are you hurt?"

She turned toward her brother, still lying there on the Stade floor, too, and opened her mouth. But not a single word came out. Her breath was spent and she felt dazed. Had he seen what had really happened? She didn't know about the others, but at this distance, it would be a near miracle if he hadn't.

Ceres heard footsteps, and suddenly two strong hands pulled her to a standing position.

"Get out now!" Brennius growled, shoving her toward the open gate to her left.

The puncture wounds in her back ached, but she forced herself back to reality and grabbed Sartes and pulled him to a standing position. Together, they darted toward the exit, trying to escape the cheers of the crowd.

They soon arrived in the dark, stuffy, tunnel, and as they did, Ceres saw dozens of combatlords inside, awaiting their turn for a few moments of glory in the arena. Some sat on benches in deep meditation, others were tensing their muscles, pumping their arms as they paced back and forth, and yet others were preparing their weapons for the imminent bloodbath. All of them, having just witnessed the fight, looked up and stared at her, curiosity in their eyes.

Ceres hurried down underground corridors lined with torches giving the gray bricks a warm glow, passing all manner of weapons leaning against the walls. She tried to ignore the pain in her back, but it was difficult to do so when with every step, the rough material in her dress chafed against the open wounds. The omnicat's claws had felt like daggers going in, but it almost seemed worse now as each gash throbbed.

"Your back is bleeding," Sartes said, a tremor in his voice.

16

"I'll be fine. We need to find Nesos and Rexus. How is your arm?"

"It hurts."

When they reached the exit, the door swung open, and two Empire soldiers stood there.

"Sartes!"

Before she could react a soldier seized her brother, and another grabbed her. It was no use resisting. The other soldier swung her over his shoulder as if she were a sack of grain, and carried her away. Fearing she had been arrested, she beat him on the back, to no avail.

Once they were just outside the Stade, he threw her onto the ground, and Sartes landed beside her. A few onlookers formed a half-circle around her, gawking, as if hungry for her blood to be spilt.

"Enter the Stade again," the soldier snarled, "and you will be hanged."

The soldiers, to her surprise, turned without another word and vanished back into the crowd.

"Ceres!" a deep voice yelled over the hum of the crowd.

Ceres looked up with relief to see Nesos and Rexus heading toward them. When Rexus threw his arms around her, she gasped. He pulled back, his eyes filled with concern.

"I'll be okay," she said.

As the throngs poured out of the Stade, Ceres and the others blended in and hurried off back into the streets, not wanting any more encounters. Walking toward Fountain Square, Ceres replayed in her mind all that had happened, still reeling. She noticed her brothers' sideways glances, and wondered what they were thinking. Had they witnessed her powers? Likely not. The omnicat had been too close. Yet at the same time they glanced at her with a new sense of respect. She wanted more than anything to tell them what had happened. Yet she knew she could not. She was not even sure herself.

There was so much unsaid between them, yet now, amidst this thick crowd, was not the time to say it. They needed to get home, and safe, first.

The streets became far less crowded the further away they traveled from the Stade. Walking next to her, Rexus took one of her hands and interlaced fingers with her.

"I'm proud of you," he said. "You saved your brother's life. I'm not sure how many sisters would do that."

He smiled, his eyes filled with compassion.

"Those wounds look deep," he remarked, glancing at her back.

"I'll be fine," she muttered.

It was a lie. She wasn't at all certain she would be fine, or that she could even make it back home. She felt quite dizzy from the blood loss, and it didn't help that her stomach rumbled, or that the sun was harassing her back, causing her to sweat bullets.

Finally, they reached Fountain Square. As soon as they walked by the booths, a merchant trailed after them, offering a large basket of food for half price.

Sartes grinned from ear to ear—which she thought was rather strange—and then he held up a copper coin with his healthy arm.

"I think I owe you some food," he said.

Ceres gasped in shock. "Where did you get that?"

"That rich girl in the golden carriage tossed out two coins, not one, but everyone was so focused on the fight between the men that they didn't even notice," Sartes replied, his smile still very much intact.

Ceres grew angry and prepared to confiscate the coin from Sartes and throw it. That was blood money, after all. They didn't need anything from rich people.

As she reached to grab it, suddenly, an old woman appeared and blocked her path.

"You!" she said, pointing at Ceres, her voice so loud Ceres felt as if it vibrated straight through her.

The woman's complexion was smooth, yet seemingly transparent, and her perfectly arched lips were tinted green. Acorns and mosses adorned her long, thick, black hair, and her brown eyes matched her long brown dress. She was beautiful to behold, Ceres thought, so much so that she became mesmerized for a moment.

Ceres blinked back, stunned, certain she had never met this woman before.

"How do you know my name?"

Her eyes locked with the woman's as she took a few steps toward her, and Ceres noticed the woman smelled heavily of myrrh.

"Vein of the stars," she said, her voice eerie.

When the woman lifted her arm in a graceful gesture, Ceres saw that a triquetra was branded on the inside of her wrist. A witch. Based on the scent of the gods, perhaps a fortune-telling one.

The woman took Ceres's rose gold hair in her hand and smelled it.

"You are no stranger to the sword," she said. "You are no stranger to the throne. Your destiny is very great, indeed. Mighty will the change be."

The woman suddenly turned and hurried away, disappearing behind her booth, and Ceres stood there, numb. She felt the woman's words penetrate her very soul. She felt that they had been more than an observation; they were a prophecy. *Mighty. Change. Throne. Destiny.* These were words she had never associated with herself before.

Could they be true? Or were they just the words of a madwoman?

Ceres looked over and saw Sartes holding a basket of food, his mouth already stuffed with more than enough bread. He held it out for her. She saw the baked good, fruits, and vegetables, and it was almost enough to break her resolve. Normally, she would have devoured it.

Yet now, for some reason, she had lost her appetite.

There was a future before her.

A destiny.

*

The walk home had taken almost an hour longer than usual, and they had all remained silent the entire way, each lost in their own thoughts. Ceres could only wonder what the people she loved most in the world thought of her. She hardly knew what to think of herself.

She looked up and saw her humble home, and she was surprised she had made it all the way, given how her head and back ached.

The others had parted with her some time ago, to run an errand for her father, and Ceres stepped alone across the creaky threshold, bracing herself, hoping she did not run into her mother.

She entered a bath of heat. She made her way over to the small vial of cleaning alcohol her mother had stored under her bed and uncorked it, careful not to use so much that it went noticed. Bracing herself for the sting, she pried her shirt and poured it down her back.

Ceres cried out from the pain, clenching her fist and leaning her head against the wall, feeling a thousand stings from the omnicat's claws. It felt as if this wound would never heal.

The door slammed open and Ceres flinched. She was relieved to see it was only Sartes.

"Father needs to see you, Ceres," he said.

Ceres noticed his eyes were slightly red.

"How's your arm?" she asked, assuming he was crying from the pain of his injured arm.

"It's not broken. Just sprained." He stepped closer and his face turned serious. "Thank you for saving me today."

She offered him a smile. "How could I be anywhere else?" she said.

He smiled.

"Go see Father now," he said. "I'll burn your dress and the cloth."

She didn't know how she'd be able to explain to her mother how her dress had suddenly vanished, but the hand-me-down definitely needed to be burned. If her mother found it in its current condition—bloodied and riddled with holes—there'd be no saying how severe her punishment would be.

Ceres left and walked down the downtrodden grass path toward the shed behind the house. There was one tree left on their humble lot—the others had been chopped into firewood and burned in the hearth to heat the house during cold winter nights—and its branches hovered over the house like a protecting energy. Every time Ceres saw it, it reminded her of her grandmother, who passed away the year before last. Her grandmother had been the one who had planted the tree when she was a child. It was her temple, in a way. And her father's too. When life was too much to handle, they would lie underneath the stars and open their hearts to Nana as if she were still alive.

Ceres entered the shed and greeted her father with a smile. To her surprise, she noticed that most of his tools had been cleared from the worktable, and that no swords waited by the hearth to be forged. She couldn't ever remember seeing the floor swept this clean, or the walls and ceiling so lacking in tools.

Her father's blue eyes lit up, the way they always did when he saw her.

"Ceres," he said, rising.

This past year, his dark hair had turned much grayer, his short beard, too, and the bags under his loving eyes had doubled in size. In the past, he had been large in stature and almost as muscular as Nesos; yet recently, Ceres noticed, he had lost weight and his formerly perfect posture was sagging.

He joined her at the door and placed a calloused hand to the small of her back.

"Walk with me."

Her chest tightened a little. When he wanted to talk *and* walk, that meant he was about to share something significant.

Side by side, they meandered to the back of the shed and into the small field. Dark clouds loomed in the near distance, sending in

20

gusts of warm, temperamental wind. She hoped they would produce the rain needed to recover from this seemingly never-ending drought, yet as before, they probably held just empty promises of showers.

The earth crunched beneath her feet as she walked, the soil dry, the plants yellow, brown, and dead. This patch of land behind their subdivision was King Claudius's, yet it hadn't been sowed for years.

They crested a hill and stopped, looking across the field. Her father remained silent, his hands clasped behind his back as he looked up into the sky. It was unlike him, and her dread deepened.

Then he spoke, seeming to select his words with care.

"Sometimes we don't have the luxury of choosing our paths," he said. "We must sacrifice all that we want for our loved ones. Even ourselves, if needed."

He sighed, and in the long silence, interrupted only by the wind, Ceres's heart pounded, wondering where he was going with this.

"What I wouldn't give to hold onto your childhood forever," he added, peering into the heavens, his face twisted in pain before it relaxed again.

"What's wrong?" Ceres asked, placing a hand on his arm.

"I must leave for a while," he said.

She felt as if she couldn't take a breath.

"Leave?"

He turned and looked her in the eyes.

"As you know, the winter and spring were particularly hard this year. The past few years of drought have been difficult. We haven't made enough money to get through the next winter, and if I don't go, our family will starve to death. I have been commissioned by another king to be his head bladesmith. It will be good money."

"You will take me with you, right?" Ceres said, a frantic tone in her voice.

He shook his head grimly.

"You must stay here and help your mother and brothers."

The thought sent a wave of horror through her.

"You can't leave me here with Mother," she said. "You wouldn't."

"I have spoken to her, and she will take care of you. She will be kind."

Ceres stomped her foot in the earth, the dust rising.

"No!"

Tears burst from her eyes and tumbled down her cheeks.

He took a small step toward her.

21

"Listen to me very carefully, Ceres. The palace still needs swords delivered from time to time. I have put in a good word for you, and if you make swords the way I have taught you, you could make a little money of your own."

Making her own money might possibly allow her more freedom. She had found her small, dainty hands had come in handy when carving intricate designs and inscriptions on the blades and hilts. Her father's hands were broad, his fingers thick and stubby, and few others had the skill she had.

Even so, she shook her head.

"I don't want to be a smith," she said.

"It runs in your blood, Ceres. And you have a gift for it."

She shook her head, adamant.

"I want to *wield* weapons," she said, "not *make* them."

As soon as the words had left her mouth, she regretted speaking them.

Her father furrowed his brow.

"You wish to be a warrior? A combatlord?"

He shook his head.

"One day it may be allowed for women to fight," she said. "You know I have practiced."

His eyebrows crinkled in worry.

"No," he commanded, firmly. "That is not your path."

Her heart sank. She felt as if her hopes and dreams of becoming a warrior were dissipating with his words. She knew he wasn't trying to be cruel—he was never cruel. It was just reality. And for them to stay alive, she would have to sacrifice her part, too.

She looked into the distance as the sky lit with a jolt of lightning. Three seconds later, thunder rumbled through the heavens.

Had she not realized how dire their circumstances were? She always assumed they would pull through together as a family, but this changed everything. Now she wouldn't have Father to hold onto, and there would be no person to stand as a shield between her and Mother.

One tear after another dropped onto the desolate earth as she remained immovable where she stood. Should she give up her dreams and follow her father's advice?

He pulled something out from behind his back, and her eyes widened to see a sword in his hand. He stepped closer, and she could see the details of the weapon.

It was awe-inspiring. The hilt was of pure gold, engraved with a serpent. The blade was two-edged and looked to be of the finest steel. Though the workmanship was foreign to Ceres, she could immediately tell it was of the finest quality. On the blade itself there was an inscription.

When heart and sword meet, there shall be the victory.

She gasped, staring at it in awe.

"Did you forge that?" she asked, her eyes glued to the sword.

He nodded.

"After the manner of the northerners," he replied. "I have labored on it for three years. Indeed, this blade alone could feed our family for an entire year."

She looked at him.

"Then why not sell it?"

He shook his head firmly.

"It wasn't made for that purpose."

He stepped closer, and to her surprise, he held it out before him.

"It was made for you."

Ceres raised a hand to her mouth and let out a moan.

"Me?" she asked, stunned.

He smiled wide.

"Did you really think I forgot your eighteenth birthday?" he replied.

She felt tears flood her eyes. She had never been more touched.

But then she thought about what he had said earlier, about not wanting her to fight, and she felt confused.

"And yet," she replied, "you said I must not train."

"I don't want you to die," he explained. "But I see where your heart is. And that, I cannot control."

He reached a hand underneath her chin and lifted her head until their eyes met.

"I am proud of you for it."

He handed her the sword, and when she felt the cool metal against her palm, she became one with it. The weight was perfect for her, and the hilt felt like it had been molded to her hand.

All the hope that had died earlier now reawakened in her chest.

"Don't tell your mother," he warned. "Hide it where she cannot find it, or she will sell it."

Ceres nodded.

"How long will you be gone?"

"I will try to be back for a visit before the first snowfall."

"That's months away!" she said, taking a step back.

"It is what I must do to—"

"No. Sell the sword. Stay!"

He placed a hand on her cheek.

"Selling this sword might help us for this season. And perhaps next. But then what?" He shook his head. "No. We need a long-term solution."

Long term? Suddenly, she realized his new job wasn't just going to be for a few months. It might be years.

Her despondency deepened.

He stepped forward, as if sensing it, and hugged her.

She felt herself begin to cry in his arms.

"I will miss you, Ceres," he said, over her shoulder. "You are different than all the others. Every day I will look up into the heavens and know you are beneath the same stars. Will you do the same?"

At first she wanted to yell at him, to say: how dare you leave me here alone.

But she felt it in her heart that he couldn't stay, and she didn't want to make it harder on him than it already was.

A tear rolled down her face. She sniffled and nodded her head.

"I will stand beneath our tree every night," she said.

He kissed her on the forehead and wrapped tender arms around her. The wounds on her back felt like knives, but she gritted her teeth and remained silent.

"I love you, Ceres."

She wanted to respond, and yet she couldn't get herself to say anything—her words were stuck in her throat.

He fetched his horse from the stable, and Ceres helped him load it with food, tools, and supplies. He embraced her one last time, and she thought her chest might burst from sadness. Yet still, she couldn't utter a single word.

He mounted the horse, and nodded before signaling to the animal to move.

Ceres waved as he rode away, and she watched with unwavering attention until he vanished behind the distant hill. The only true love she had ever known came from that man. And now he was gone.

Rain started to descend from the heavens, and it prickled against her face.

"Father!" she screamed as loudly as she could. "Father, I love you!"

She fell to her knees and buried her hands in her face, sobbing.

Life, she knew, would never be the same again.

CHAPTER THREE

With aching feet and burning lungs, Ceres climbed the steep hill as swiftly as she could without spilling a drop of water from either bucket by her sides. Normally she would pause for a break, but her mother had threatened no breakfast unless she was back by sunrise—and no breakfast meant she wouldn't eat until dinner. She didn't mind the pain, anyway—it, at least, allowed her to take her mind off her father, and the miserable new state of things since he had left.

The sun was just now cresting the Alva Mountains in the distance, painting the scattered clouds above golden-pink, and soft wind sighed through the tall, yellow grass on either side of the road. Ceres drew the fresh morning air in through her nose and willed herself faster. Her mother wouldn't find it an acceptable excuse that their regular well had dried up, or that there was a long line at the other one a half a mile away. Indeed, she did not stop until she reached the top of the hill—and once she did, she stopped in her tracks, stunned at the sight before her.

There, in the distance, was her house—and before it sat a bronze wagon. Her mother stood before it, conversing with a man who was so overweight, Ceres thought she had never seen anyone even half his size. He wore a burgundy linen tunic and a red silk hat, and his long beard was bushy and gray. She squinted, trying to understand. Was he a merchant?

Her mother was wearing her best dress, a green linen floor-length gown she had purchased years ago with money that was supposed to be used to buy Ceres new shoes. None of this made any sense.

Hesitantly, Ceres started down the hill. She kept her eyes trained on them, and when she saw the old man hand her mother a heavy leather pouch, saw her mother's emaciated face light up, she grew even more curious. Had their misfortune turned? Would Father be able to return home? The thoughts made her chest lighten a little, although she wouldn't allow herself to feel any excitement until she learned the details.

When Ceres neared their house, her mother turned and smiled at her warmly—and immediately Ceres felt a knot of worry in her stomach. The last time her mother had smiled at her like that—teeth gleaming, eyes bright—Ceres had received a flogging.

25

"Darling daughter," her mother said in an overly sweet tone, opening her arms toward her with a grin that made Ceres's blood curdle.

"*This* is the girl?" the old man said with an eager smile, his dark, beady eyes widening when he looked at Ceres.

Now up close, Ceres could see every wrinkle on the obese man's skin. His broad flat nose seemed to overtake his entire face, and when he took off his hat, his sweaty bald head glowed in the sunlight.

Her mother waltzed over to Ceres, took the buckets from her, and set them on the singed grass. That gesture alone confirmed to Ceres that something was severely wrong. She began to feel a panicky sensation rise in her chest.

"Meet my pride and joy, my only daughter, Ceres," her mother said, pretending to wipe a tear away from her eye when there was none. "Ceres, this is Lord Blaku. Please show your respects to your new master."

A jolt of fear stabbed Ceres through the chest. She sucked in a sudden breath. Ceres looked at her mother, and with her back to Lord Blaku, her mother gave her a smile that was as evil as she had ever seen.

"*Master?*" Ceres asked.

"To save our family from financial ruin and public embarrassment, the benevolent Lord Blaku offered your father and me a generous deal: a sack of gold in exchange for you."

"What?" Ceres gasped, feeling herself sinking into the earth.

"Now, be the good girl I know you are and show your respects," her mother said, shooting Ceres a warning glance.

"I will not," Ceres said, taking a step back as she puffed her chest up, feeling silly for not having immediately realized the man was a slaver, and that the transaction was for her life.

"Father would never sell me," she added through clenched teeth, her horror and indignation rising.

Her mother scowled and grabbed her by the arm, her fingernails digging into Ceres's skin.

"If you behave, this man might take you as his wife, and for you, that is a very lucky thing," she muttered.

Lord Blaku licked his thin crusty lips as his puffy eyes greedily wandered up and down Ceres's body. How could her mother do this to her? She knew her mother didn't love her as much as her brothers—but this?

"Marita," he said in a nasally voice. "You told me your daughter was fair, but you neglected to tell me what an utterly magnificent creature she is. Dare I say, I have yet to see a woman with lips as succulent as hers, and with eyes as passionate, and with a body as firm and exquisite."

Ceres's mother placed a hand over her heart with a sigh, and Ceres felt like she might just vomit right here. She clenched her hands into fists as she snapped her arm away from her mother's grasp.

"Perhaps I should have asked for more, if she pleases you so much," Ceres's mother said, her eyes lowering in despondency. "She is, after all, our only beloved girl."

"I am willing to pay good money for such a beauty. Will another five gold pieces suffice?" he asked.

"How generous of you," her mother replied.

Lord Blaku ambled over to his wagon to fetch more gold.

"Father will never agree to this," Ceres sneered.

Ceres's mother took a threatening step toward her.

"Oh, but it was your father's idea," her mother snapped, with her eyebrows raised halfway up her forehead. Ceres knew she was lying now—whenever she did that, she was lying.

"Do you actually think your father loves you more than he loves me?" her mother asked.

Ceres blinked, wondering what that would have to do with anything.

"I could never love someone who thinks she is better than me," she added.

"You never loved me?" Ceres asked, her anger morphing into hopelessness.

With the gold in hand, Lord Blaku waddled over to Ceres's mother and handed it to her.

"Your daughter is worth every piece," he said. "She will be a good wife and bear me many sons."

Ceres bit the inside of her lips and shook her head over and over again.

"Lord Blaku will come for you in the morning, so go inside and pack your belongings," Ceres's mother said.

"I won't!" Ceres screamed.

"That was always your problem, girl. You only ever think of yourself. This gold," her mother said, jingling the purse in front of Ceres's face, "will keep your brothers alive. It will keep our family intact, allowing us to remain in our home and make repairs. Did you fail to think about that?"

For a split second, Ceres thought maybe she was being selfish, but then she realized her mother was playing mind games again, using Ceres's love for her brothers against her.

"Do not worry," Ceres's mother said, turning toward Lord Blaku. "Ceres will comply. All you need to do is be firm with her, and she becomes as meek as a lamb."

Never. Never would she be that man's wife or anyone's property. And never would she let her mother or anyone exchange her life for fifty-five pieces of gold.

"I will never go with this slaver," Ceres snapped, shooting him a look of disgust.

"Ungrateful child!" Ceres's mother yelled. "If you do not do as I say, I will beat you so severely you will never walk again. Now get inside!"

The thought of being beaten by her mother brought back awful, visceral memories; she was taken back to that dreadful moment at five years old when her mother had beaten her until everything had gone black. The wounds from that beating and many others healed—yet the wounds in Ceres's heart had never stopped bleeding. And now that she knew for sure that her mother didn't love her, and never had, her heart split wide open for good.

Before she could respond, Ceres's mother stepped forward and slapped her across the face so hard her ear began ringing.

At first, Ceres was stunned by the sudden assault, and she almost backed down. But then something snapped inside her. She would not allow herself to cower as she always did.

Ceres smacked her mother back, across the cheek, so hard that she tumbled to the ground, gasping in horror.

Red-faced, her mother climbed to her feet, grabbed Ceres by the shoulder and hair, and kneed Ceres in the stomach. When Ceres stooped forward in agony, her mother jabbed her knee into Ceres's face, causing her to fall to the ground.

The slaver stood and watched, his eyes wide, chuckling, clearly taking delight in the fight.

Still coughing and gasping for air from the assault, Ceres staggered to her feet. Screaming, she flung herself toward her mother, driving her to the ground.

This ends today, was all Ceres could think. All the years of never being loved, of being treated with disdain, fueled her rage. Ceres smashed closed fists into her mother's face again and again as tears of fury rolled down her cheeks, sobs uncontrollably spilling out of her lips.

Finally, her mother went limp.

28

Ceres's shoulders shook with each cry, her insides wrung inside out. Blurred by tears, she looked up at the slaver with an even more intense hatred.

"You will make a good one," Lord Blaku said with a guileful grin, as he picked up the bag of gold from the ground and attached it to his leather belt.

Before she could react, suddenly his hands were upon her. He grabbed Ceres and climbed into the carriage, tossing her into the back in one quick motion, as if she were a bag of potatoes. His massive bulk and strength was too much for her to resist. Holding her wrist with one arm and taking hold of a chain with the other, he said, "I'm not stupid enough to think you would still be here in morning."

She glanced at the house that had been her home for eighteen years, and her eyes filled with tears as she thought of her brothers and her father. But she had to make a choice if she was to save herself, before the chain was around her ankle.

So in one quick motion, she mustered all of her strength and snatched her arm out of the slaver's grip, lifted her leg, and kicked him in the face as hard as she could. He fell backwards, out of the carriage, and tumbled onto the ground.

She jumped from the wagon and ran as fast as she could down the dirt road, away from the woman she vowed to never call mother again, away from everything she had ever known and loved.

CHAPTER FOUR

Surrounded by the royal family, Thanos tried hard to keep a pleasant expression on his face as he gripped the gold wine goblet—yet he could not. He hated being here. He hated these people, his family. And he hated attending royal gatherings—especially the ones following the Killings. He knew how the people lived, how poor they were, and he felt how senseless and unjust all this pomp and haughtiness really was. He would give anything to be far away from here.

Standing with his cousins Lucious, Aria, and Varius, Thanos didn't make the least bit of effort to engage in their petty conversation. Instead, he watched the imperial guests meander about in the palace gardens, wearing their togas and stolas, presenting fake grins and spewing false niceties. A few of his cousins were throwing food at each other as they ran across the manicured lawn and between tables stocked with food and wine. Others were reenacting their favorite scenes from the Killings, laughing at and mocking those who had lost their lives today.

Hundreds of people, Thanos thought, and not one was honorable.

"Next month, I will purchase three combatlords," Lucious, the eldest, said in a boisterous tone as he patted drops of sweat from his brow with a silk handkerchief. "Stefanus wasn't worth half of what I paid for him, and if he weren't dead already, I would have run a sword through him myself for having fought like a girl in the first round."

Aria and Varius laughed, but Thanos didn't find his comment amusing. Whether they considered the Killings a game or not, they should respect the brave and the dead.

"Well, did you see Brennius?" Aria asked, her large blue eyes widening. "I actually considered buying him, but he gave me this conceited look when I watched him rehearse. Can you believe it?" she added, as she rolled her eyes and huffed.

"And he stinks like a skunk," Lucious added.

Everyone except for Thanos laughed again.

"None of us would have picked him," Varius said. "Though he lasted longer than expected, his form was horrible."

Thanos couldn't keep quiet another second.

"Brennius had the best form in the entire arena," he interjected. "Don't talk about the art of combat as if you know anything about it."

The cousins grew quiet, and Aria's eyes became large as saucers as she looked toward the ground. Varius puffed out his chest and crossed his arms, scowling. He stepped closer to Thanos as if to challenge him, and the air thickened with tension.

"Well, never mind those self-important combatlords," Aria said, stepping between them, defusing the situation. She waved for the boys to gather around closer, and then she whispered, "I have heard an outlandish rumor. A little bee told me the king wants to have someone of royal birth compete in the Killings."

They all exchanged an uncomfortable look as they fell silent.

"Perhaps," Lucious said. "It won't be me, though. I'm not willing to risk my life for a stupid game."

Thanos knew he could beat out most combatlords, but killing another human wasn't something he wanted to do.

"You're just scared of dying," Aria said.

"I am not," Lucious retorted. "You take that back!"

Thanos's patience was spent. He walked away.

Thanos watched his distant cousin Stephania wander about as if she were looking for someone—probably him. A few weeks back, the Queen had said he was fated to be with Stephania, but Thanos felt otherwise. Stephania was as spoiled as the rest of the cousins and he'd rather give up his name, his inheritance, and even his sword to not have to marry her. She was beautiful to behold, true— her hair golden, her skin milky white, her lips blood-red—but if he had to listen to her talk about how life was so unfair one more time, he thought he might cut his ears off.

He scurried to the outskirts of the garden toward the rose bushes, avoiding eye contact with any of the attendees. But just as he rounded the corner, Stephania stepped in front of him, her brown eyes lighting up.

"Good evening, Thanos," she said with a scintillating smile that would have most of the boys here drooling after her. Everyone but Thanos.

"Good evening to you, too," Thanos said and skirted around her, continuing to walk.

She lifted up her stola and trailed after him like a pesky mosquito.

"Don't you find it so unfair how—" she began.

"I'm busy," Thanos snapped in a tone harsher than he intended, causing her to gasp. He then turned toward her. "I'm sorry...I'm just tired of all these parties."

"Perhaps you would like to stroll the gardens with me?" Stephania said, her right eyebrow peaking as she stepped closer.

That was the absolute last thing he wanted.

"Listen," he said, "I know the queen and your mother have it in their minds that we somehow belong together, but—"

"Thanos!" he heard behind him.

Thanos turned to see the king's messenger.

"The king would like you to join him in the gazebo straightaway," he said. "And you too, my lady."

"Might I inquire why?" Thanos asked.

"There is much to discuss," the messenger said.

Not having had regular conversations with the king in the past, Thanos wondered what that might entail.

"Of course," Thanos said.

To his great dismay, a beaming Stephania hooked her arm around his, and together they followed the messenger over to the gazebo.

When Thanos noticed several of the king's advisors and even the crown prince already sitting on benches and chairs, he found it odd that he had been invited, too. He would hardly have anything of value to offer in their conversation, as his opinions about how the Empire was ruled differed greatly from those of everyone here. The best thing he could do, he thought to himself, was to keep his mouth shut.

"What a lovely couple you make," the queen said with a warm smile as they entered.

Thanos pinched his lips shut and offered Stephania to sit down next to him.

Once everyone had settled, the king rose to his feet and the gathering quieted down. His uncle wore a knee-length toga, but where the others were white, red, and blue, his was purple, a color reserved only for the king. Around his balding temple was a golden wreath, and his cheeks and eyes still drooped even though he was smiling.

"The masses grow unruly," he said, his voice grave, slow. He slowly scanned all the faces with the authority of a king. "The time is past due to remind them who is king and enact harsher rules. From this day forward, I shall double tithes on all property and food."

There came a surprised murmur, followed by nods of approval.

"An excellent choice, your grace," said one of his advisors.

Thanos couldn't believe his ears. Double the people's taxes? Having mingled with commoners, he knew that the taxes required were already beyond what most commoners could afford. He had seen mothers mourn the loss of their children who died of starvation. As recently as yesterday, he had offered food to a homeless four-year-old girl whose every bone was visible beneath her skin.

Thanos had to look away or he would surely have to speak up against this insanity.

"And finally," the king said, "from now on, to counterbalance the underground revolution that is fomenting, the firstborn son in every family will become a servant in the king's army."

One after another, the small crowd commended the king for his wise decision.

Finally, though, Thanos felt the king turn to him.

"Thanos," the king finally said. "You have remained silent. Speak!"

Silence fell on the gazebo, as all eyes were on Thanos. He stood. He knew he had to speak up, for the emaciated girl, for the grieving mothers, for the voiceless whose lives seemed not to matter. He needed to represent them, because if he did not, no one would.

"Harsher rules will not crush the rebellion," he said, his heart thumping in his chest. "It will only embolden it. Instilling fear into the citizens and denying them freedom will do nothing but compel them to rise against us and join the revolution."

A few people laughed, while others talked amongst themselves. Stephania took his hand and tried to hush him, but he snatched it away.

"A great king uses love, as well as fear, to rule his subordinates," Thanos said.

The king gave the queen an uneasy glance. He stood up, and then walked over to Thanos.

"Thanos, you are a brave young man for speaking up," he said, placing a hand on his shoulder. "However, was your younger brother not murdered in cold blood by these same people, those who governed themselves, as you say?"

Thanos saw red. How dare his uncle bring up his brother's death so flippantly? For years, Thanos had fallen asleep to his grief as he mourned the loss of his brother.

"Those who murdered my brother didn't have enough food for themselves," Thanos said. "A desperate man will seek desperate measures."

"Do you question the king's wisdom?" the queen asked.

Thanos couldn't believe no one else was speaking up against this. Did they see not see how unjust it was? Did they not realize these new laws would breathe fire into the rebellion?

"Not for a moment will you be able to fool the people into believing you want anything other than their suffering and your profiting for yourselves," Thanos said.

There came a gasp of disapproval amidst the group.

"You speak harsh words, nephew," the king said, looking him in the eyes. "I would almost believe you mean to join the rebellion."

"Or perhaps he is already a part of it?" the queen said, her eyebrows rising.

"I am not," Thanos barked.

The air in the gazebo grew hotter, and Thanos realized if he wasn't careful, he might be accused of treason—a crime punishable by death without trial.

Stephania stood up and took Thanos's hand in hers—yet, agitated by her timing, he snapped his hand away.

Stephania's expression fell, and she looked down.

"Perhaps in time you will see the weaknesses of your beliefs," the king said to Thanos. "For now, our ruling will stand and shall be implemented immediately."

"Good," the queen said with a sudden smile. "Now, let us move onto the second item on our agenda. Thanos, as a young man of nineteen, we, your imperial sovereigns, have chosen a wife for you. We have decided you and Stephania are to be wed."

Thanos glanced over at Stephania, whose eyes were glazed with tears, an expression of worry painting her face. He felt aghast. How could they demand this of him?

"I cannot marry her," Thanos whispered, a knot forming in his belly.

Murmurs went through the crowd, and the queen shot to her feet so quickly that her chair fell backward with a crack.

"Thanos!" she yelled, hands clenched by her sides. "How dare you defy the king? You will marry Stephania whether or not you want to."

Thanos looked at Stephania with saddened eyes as tears rolled down her cheeks.

"Do you imagine you are too good for me?" she asked, her bottom lip trembling.

He took a step toward Stephania to comfort her what little he could, but before he reached her, she ran out of the gazebo, hands covering her face as she cried.

The king stood, clearly angered.

"Deny her, son", he said, his voice suddenly cold and hard, thundering through the gazebo, "and it will be the dungeon for you."

CHAPTER FIVE

Ceres sprinted, weaving through city streets, until she felt her legs would no longer hold her, until her lungs burned so much they might burst, and until she knew with absolute certainty the slaver would never find her.

Finally, she collapsed on the ground in a back alley amongst garbage and rats, arms wrapped around her legs, tears streaming down her hot cheeks. With her father away and her mother wanting to sell her, she had no one. If she remained on the streets and slept in the alleys, she would eventually die of starvation or freeze to death when winter came. Perhaps that would be best.

For hours she sat and cried, her eyes puffy, her mind muddled with despair. Where would she go now? How would she make money to survive?

The day had grown long when finally, she resolved to return home, sneak into the shed, take the few swords that were left, and sell them to the palace. They were expecting her today anyway. That way, she would have money for a few days at least until she could come up with a better plan.

She would also pick up the sword her father had given her and that she had hidden beneath the floorboards in the shed. But she wouldn't sell that, no. Not until she was staring death in the face would she give up her father's gift.

She jogged home, carefully watching for any familiar faces or for the slaver's wagon as she went. When she reached the last hill, she slunk behind the row of houses and into the field, tiptoeing across the parched earth, her eyes scanning for her mother.

A pang of guilt arose when she remembered how she had beaten her mother. She never wanted to hurt her, not even after how cruel her mother had been. Not even with her heart broken and unmendable.

Arriving at the back of their shed, she peeked in through a crack in the wall. Seeing it was empty, she stepped inside the dim shack and gathered the swords. But just as she was about to lift the floorboard where she had hidden the sword, she heard voices coming from outside.

When she stood up and glanced through a small hole in the wall, to her horror, she saw her mother and Sartes walking toward the shed. Her mother had a black eye and a bruise on her cheek, and now seeing her mother alive and well, it almost made Ceres smile knowing she had put it there. All the anger welled up again as she thought about how her mother wanted to sell her.

"If I catch you sneaking any food out to Ceres, I will flog you, do you understand?" her mother snapped as she and Sartes strode by her grandmother's tree.

When Sartes didn't answer, her mother slapped him across the face.

"Do you understand, boy?" she said.

"Yes," Sartes said, looking down, a tear in his eye.

"And if you ever see her, bring her home so I can give her a licking she will never forget."

They began walking toward the shed again, and Ceres's heart was suddenly thumping wildly. She gripped the swords and darted toward the back door as quickly and as quietly as she could. Just as she exited, the front door swung open, and she leaned against the outer wall and listened, the wounds from the omnicat's claws stinging her back.

"Who goes there?" her mother said.

Ceres held her breath and squeezed her eyes shut.

"I know you're there," her mother said and waited. "Sartes, go check the back door. It's ajar."

Ceres clenched the swords to her chest. She heard Sartes's footsteps as he walked toward her, and then the door opened with a creak.

Sartes's eyes widened when he saw her, and he gasped.

"Is there anyone there?" her mother asked.

"Um... no," Sartes said, his eyes filling with tears as they connected with Ceres's.

Ceres mouthed a "thank you," and Sartes gestured with his hand for her to leave.

She nodded, and with a heavy heart, she stole toward the field as the back door to the shed slammed shut. She would come back for her sword later.

*

Ceres stopped at the palace gates sweating, famished, and exhausted, swords in hand. The Empire soldiers standing guard, clearly recognizing her as the girl who delivered her father's swords, let her pass without questioning her.

She hurried through the cobblestone courtyard and then turned for the blacksmith's stone cottage behind one of the four towers. She entered.

Standing by the anvil in front of the crackling furnace, the blacksmith hammered away at a glowing blade, the leather apron protecting his clothing from the flying sparks. The concerned expression on his face made Ceres wonder what was wrong. A jovial middle-aged man full of energy, he was rarely worried.

His bald, sweaty head greeted her before he noticed she had entered.

"Good morrow," he said when he saw her, nodding for her to place the swords on the worktable.

She strode across the hot smoky room and set them down, the metal rattling against a surface of burnt, tattered wood.

He shook his head, clearly troubled.

"What is it?" she asked.

He looked up, concern in his eyes.

"Of all the days to fall ill," he murmured.

"Bartholomew?" she asked, seeing that the young weapon-keeper of the combatlords wasn't here as he usually was, frantically preparing the last few weapons before sparring practice.

The blacksmith stopped hammering and looked up with a vexed expression, his bushy eyebrows crinkling.

He shook his head.

"And on sparring day, of all days," he said. "And not just any sparring day." He stuffed the blade into the glowing coals in the furnace and wiped his dripping brow with the sleeve of his tunic. "Today, the royals will spar with the combatlords. The king has hand-picked twelve royals to train for the Killings. Three will go on to participate."

She understood his worry. It was his responsibility to provide the weapon-keepers, and if he didn't, his job was on the line. Hundreds of blacksmiths would be eager to take his position.

"The king won't be happy if we are one weapon-keeper short," she said.

He leaned his hands on his thick thighs and shook his head. Just then, two Empire soldiers entered.

"We are here to retrieve the weapons," one said, scowling toward Ceres.

Even though it wasn't forbidden, she knew it was frowned upon for girls to work in weaponry—a man's field. Yet she had grown accustomed to snide remarks and hateful glares most every time she made deliveries to the palace.

The blacksmith stood up and walked over to three wooden buckets filled with weapons, all ready for the sparring match.

"You will find here the remainder of the weapons the king requested for today," the blacksmith said to the Empire soldiers.

"And the weapon-keeper?" the Empire soldier demanded.

Just as the blacksmith opened his mouth to speak, Ceres had an idea.

"It is me," she said, excitement rising in her chest. "I am the stand-in today and until Bartholomew returns."

The Empire soldiers looked at her for a moment, startled.

Ceres pinched her lips together and took a step forward.

"I have been working with my father and with the palace my entire life, crafting swords, shields, and all manner of weapons," she said.

She didn't know where her courage came from, but she stood tall and stared the soldiers in the eye.

"Ceres…" the blacksmith said, giving her a look of pity.

"Try me," she said, strengthening her resolve, wanting them to test her abilities. "There isn't anyone who can take Bartholomew's place but me. And if you lack a weapon-keeper today, wouldn't that make the king rather upset?"

She wasn't certain, but she figured the Empire soldiers and the blacksmith would do almost anything to keep the king happy. Especially today.

The Empire soldiers looked at the blacksmith, and the blacksmith back at them. The blacksmith thought for a moment. And then another. Finally, he nodded. He laid a plethora of weapons onto the table, after which he gestured to her to proceed.

"Show us, then, Ceres," the blacksmith said, a twinkle in his eye. "Knowing your father, he probably taught you everything you are not supposed to know."

"And more," Ceres said, smiling inside.

She went over each weapon, explaining in great detail their uses and advantages, how one might be better in certain types of battles than others.

When she was finished, the Empire soldiers looked to the blacksmith.

"I suppose it is better to have a girl weapon-keeper than no weapon-keeper," the blacksmith said. "Let us go and speak to the king. Perhaps he will allow it, seeing there is no other."

Ceres was so excited she almost threw her arms around the blacksmith as he winked at her. The soldiers still seemed reluctant, but with no other apparent option, they agreed to take her along.

She followed the Empire soldiers out the back door and entered the palace training ground. Ceres was used to the sound of swords colliding, of the combatlords grunting as they sparred, and of the smell of sweat mixed with leather and metal filling the air. But what was quite unique was seeing the royals practicing in the center of the yard, wearing their fancy polished armor, looking as if they needed a lesson—or a hundred—in swordsmanship. Ceres didn't feel they belonged here. No, it disgusted her to see them on the training ground, all the underlords, counts, and dignitaries watching as they ate from mounds of food and drank from golden goblets. They should go back to their lavish parties, she thought. Not feign courage and honor.

One of the royals, though, stood out from the rest: Thanos. Watching him spar, she noticed how he moved with speed, grace, and agility. To her surprise, he appeared almost as skilled as Brennius; and he wore no armor like the other royals. His hair was different from his royal peers', too; not neat and pulled back into a low ponytail, but curly, unruly dark hair flying about his face with each move.

Ceres frowned. Perhaps he knew a thing or two about combat, but he was the haughtiest of the royals, always glowering at something or someone, never seeming to want to be a part of anything.

The guards led her to the throne, and when the blacksmith presented Ceres to the king as a stand-in weapon-keeper, the king paused, and then chuckled a bit as he glanced at his advisors on either side. Ceres didn't like how he looked at her as if she were an annoyance to be rid of. But in an instant, the king's expression changed, and his face lit up as if he just had the most brilliant idea.

"Not having anyone else, I see that this must be as you say," the king said to the blacksmith. "Ceres, you shall assist Prince Thanos."

The king said it in a way that made Ceres think it was a punishment or a means to shame Prince Thanos, but she didn't care. Even though she wasn't particularly happy to be Thanos's weapon-keeper, she had been assigned, and now she could show her skills in the royal court. It was more than any girl could ever expect.

She bowed toward the king and glanced at the blacksmith as she passed him. The blacksmith nodded, an almost prideful expression on his face, and then he walked back to the chalet.

The Empire soldier escorted Ceres over to Thanos, who stood by a table, and when Thanos glanced at Ceres, his scowl intensified.

"Very well," he muttered, staring at his uncle across the yard as if daggers were shooting from his eyes. The king gave Thanos a devious smirk, affirming to Ceres that her assignment to Thanos was indeed some form of a punishment.

Thanos stepped in front of Ceres, and she noticed how the neck of his shirt was open, revealing small amounts of curly, dark hair on his muscular chest. Her breath hitched. He looked at her, and when their eyes met, she found his gaze intense—irises darker than the blackest soot. Yet, he didn't intimidate her. In fact, his bottomless eyes drew her to him, making it impossible to look away.

Once he broke eye contact, Ceres was able to take a breath and think clearly; she again resolved to show him she knew what she was doing.

"I suppose I should trust you if the blacksmith speaks so highly of you," Thanos said as she laid out the weapons one by one onto the wooden table.

Even though she was a girl, and even though Thanos was undoubtedly smart enough to figure out that what his uncle had done was more of a cruel joke than anything, it surprised her that he gave her the benefit of the doubt.

"I will do my best, sire," she said, placing a sword onto the wood.

He glanced at her, his smoldering eyes studying her too intimately for her to feel comfortable.

"There is no need for such formalities here. Thanos will do," he said.

Again, she was surprised by his casual approach. Had she read him wrong? Was he not the arrogant, self-righteous, ungrateful young man she assumed he was?

Once she had laid out all the weapons, an Empire soldier reviewed the rules of combat. First, they watched a few of the combatlords spar, and then it was the royals' turn. The Empire soldier called upon Lucious, a blond, muscular, but somewhat lanky young man, who stepped up to a combatlord. Thanos leaned over.

"I doubt Lucious will last very long," he whispered.

"Why do you say that?" Ceres asked, wondering why he would say something like that to her—a stranger—about a fellow royal.

"You'll see."

The right side of Thanos's lips rose, and Ceres liked how he spoke to her as if she were an equal.

Even before the fighting began, Ceres knew Thanos was right. Lucious's feet were too close together, his grip weak around the hilt, and his eyes too unfocused. It would be an embarrassment, to say the least, to watch him lose rather quickly to such a warrior he was facing.

With the first collision of swords, Ceres looked up and kept her gaze on the cloudy sky instead, keeping them there as she heard grunts and blades clashing. The fighting continued on for a while, and Ceres wondered if perhaps she had judged Lucious too harshly. At least Lucious was holding on, if nothing else.

But when Lucious started to scream a few minutes into the fight, and the onlookers murmured and gasped, she couldn't help but bring her eyes back onto the fighters again. Lucious was lying on the ground, holding the blade of his sword with one hand, the hilt with the other, struggling to keep the combatlord's sword away from his face. Blood ran down his arm, and he squealed, begging for the round to end.

"Enough!" the king said, and the combatlord retreated.

Lucious's weapon-keeper ran over to him and offered him a hand, but Lucious smacked it away.

"I can get up myself!" he yelled between gritted teeth, panting and spewing obscenities.

Lucious held his injured hand with the other and rolled onto his stomach before rising to his feet.

"I said I didn't want to do this!" he yelled toward the king. "And now look what happened! You have made me a fool!"

He stormed across the yard and vanished through the arching doorway into the palace. Most of the dignitaries had quieted, but some of them laughed

"Always such drama with Lucious," Thanos said, rolling his eyes.

"Next up is Thanos and Oedifus," an Empire soldier announced.

"Are you ready?" Thanos asked Ceres.

"Yes. Are you?" she replied.

He paused and gave her a sideways glance before saying, "Always. Let me start with the trident and shield."

She handed him the shield, and after he had secured it onto his arm, she gave him the trident. Her pulse rose as she watched him walk into the center of the practice arena, hoping he would win, but bracing herself in the very likely event he would lose. One did not just simply triumph over a combatlord, and especially not with as little training as Ceres assumed these royals had.

The combatlord was around Thanos's height, but his muscles were fuller, almost monstrously so, Ceres observed. His arms were covered in scars, his face disfigured from past wounds unevenly healed, and he grunted at Thanos even before the match had begun.

With Thanos's very first strike, Ceres could tell he was a marvelous warrior, and as the battle continued, as hard as he tried, the combatlord couldn't get to him. Thanos was so quick to swerve, and quick like a rattlesnake to attack, but he also possessed the strength of an omnicat. Not only did he seem to read his opponent's mind, his feet moved with the ease of a trained dancer.

The entire match, Thanos was one step ahead of the combatlord, causing the onlookers to cheer with excitement. Ceres judged the trident a great choice for him, but from the way he moved, she believed a longsword would be the weapon granting him victory.

With the next move, the combatlord crouched and whipped one leg across the sand in a circular motion, wiping Thanos's feet from under him, causing him to fall onto his back. He hopped up to his feet again, but his trident had fallen several feet away.

Faster than she could even think, Ceres picked up the longsword and yelled, "Thanos!"

He glanced at her and she threw the sword to him. Catching it mid-air, Thanos didn't miss a beat and went after the combatlord with full force. Sparks flew as metal collided with metal, and watching Thanos's face and neck muscles strain, Ceres clenched her fists as she held her breath.

Retreating, the combatlord snarled and panted, saliva gushing from his mouth, but Thanos did not withdraw. Instead, he hit the combatlord's sword out of his hand and shoved him to the ground so Thanos ended up standing above him with his blade pointed at his challenger's neck.

With eyes wide open and her heart galloping in her chest, Ceres cheered with the rest of the crowd.

Thanos looked up at the king, his face a stone, and the king squinted his eyes as he leaned over and whispered something to the advisor on his right. With the nod of his uncle, Thanos lowered his sword and stepped out of the training area.

He walked toward her, a new look of admiration and wonder in his eyes. He studied her in silence for several seconds, breathing hard. Finally, he spoke.

"How did you know which weapon to give me?" he asked, wiping the sweat from his brow with a handkerchief.

"The way you moved," she said. "It seemed a longsword would suit you."

Still panting, he watched her closely as he nodded.

Then he strode across the training ground and headed into the palace. For a moment, Ceres wasn't certain what to make of his strange behavior and his lack of further instructions. Should she stay? Should she leave? She decided to wait until she was released.

A few minutes later, and into the next round, a handler approached her.

"For you, my lady," he said, holding out a pouch. "An advance from Prince Thanos. If you accept, you have been hired as the prince's new weapon-keeper. He requests you return tomorrow an hour after dawn at this very spot."

Ceres held out her hand and after she had received the pouch, she opened it, seeing five pieces of gold. At first, overwrought with joy, she couldn't speak, but when the handler asked her again if she would accept, she said yes.

"You are at liberty to leave, my lady," he said, and then he swiveled around and walked back into the palace.

"Thank you," she said, realizing she was speaking to no one. She glanced up toward the east tower and saw Thanos standing on the balcony watching her. He nodded to her and smiled before heading inside.

With a light heart, she ran from the palace and headed home to pick up her sword. She also planned to secretly give the money to her brothers without their mother finding out, and to bid them a final farewell.

Finally, she was wanted.

Finally, she had a home.

CHAPTER SIX

Ceres carefully peered in through the half-opened shutters, her mouth dry, eyes peeled for her mother. She had run home as nightfall descended on Delos, the clear skies above turning pink and lavender. Her eagerness to present the gold to her brothers had fueled each step. Aching with hunger, she had considered using one of the gold coins to purchase food, but was afraid to bump into her mother at the market.

With ears pinned for sounds or voices, she glanced further into the dim house. Not a soul was in sight. Where could Nesos and Sartes be? Usually, they were home at this time while Mother was away. Perhaps if she retrieved her sword first, her brothers would return by then.

Careful not to make a sound, she slunk around to the rear of the house, past her grandmother's tree and toward the shed. The door creaked when she opened it, and once inside the stuffy shack, she headed straight toward the corner. Kneeling down beside the floorboard, she lifted it up and fished out her sword. She breathed with relief to see it was still there.

For a moment Ceres sat and admired its beauty, the mixed metals, the shiny, thin, unblemished blade, the golden hilt adorned with serpents. The craftsmanship was after the manner of the northerners, her father had said. She would carry this sword with honor, always remembering the great love her father had for her.

She slid it into its sheath, secured it around her waist with a scabbard, and headed outside.

Seeing no one was there, she made her way to the front of the house again, and this time went in through the front door. The house was shadowy, the hearth unlit, and mounds of fruits, vegetables, meats, and baked goods decked the table, all no doubt bought with the gold gained by selling her life. Their savory aroma filled the room. She strode over to the food, picked up a loaf of bread, and devoured a few bites. Her stomach had churned for days.

Knowing she hadn't much time, Ceres hurried over to Nesos's bench-bed and placed the sack of gold beneath his pillow. He'd find it when he turned in for the night, and she didn't doubt he'd keep it a secret from Mother. She blinked, trying to fight back the tears while wondering if she'd ever see her dear brothers again. Her heart squeezed as she thought about Rexus. Would he forget about her?

Suddenly she jumped as the front door flung open, startling her. To her horror, in stepped Lord Blaku.

He grinned an awful, victorious grin.

"If it isn't the runaway," he said, his upper lip curled back, revealing yellowing teeth, the stench of sweat saturating the room.

Taking a few steps back, Ceres realized she needed to get away—quick. Thinking she'd be able to escape through the window in her parents' bedroom, she dropped the loaf of bread and darted toward the back door.

But just as she reached the doorway, her mother stepped into it, Ceres colliding with her.

Briefly, Ceres noted that her mother wore a new dress made of the finest silk, and that she smelled like floral perfume.

"Did you really think you could beat me bloody and blue, steal my money, and get away with it?" her mother asked in a hateful tone as she grabbed Ceres's hair, pulling it so hard Ceres let out a cry.

Steal her money? But then it all made sense. Of course her mother wouldn't be collaborating with the slaver if she knew he had taken back the gold he'd paid for Ceres. However, he probably told her mother Ceres took the gold and ran off with it. Her mother was, after all, unconscious when he snatched the pouch of fifty-five pieces.

Before Ceres could explain, her mother slapped her across the face and shoved her so she fell to the floor. She then kicked Ceres in the stomach with her new pointy shoes.

Ceres couldn't breathe. Yet she forced herself to her feet, preparing to lunge for her mother—when the slaver grabbed her from behind in a deadlock. He squeezed her so hard she was certain the wounds on her back reopened.

She kicked and screamed, wriggled and scratched, trying to wrestle her way out of the fat old man's iron grip. But it was to no avail. He carried her through the room, and toward the front door.

"Wait!" her mother yelled.

She walked over to them and wrapped covetous fingers around Ceres's sword.

"What is this?" she asked, her eyes angered.

Still not giving up the fight, Ceres kicked her mother in the shin as hard as she could muster with the slaver squeezing the life out of her.

Her mother's face turned red, and she socked Ceres in the abdomen with such force Ceres thought she might vomit up the little food she had managed to swallow.

"That is *my* sword," her mother said.

Ceres knew her mother would recognize how valuable the sword was, and that there was no way she would let the slaver take it with him.

"I paid for the girl, and whatever is on her person, I own that now," Lord Blaku sneered.

"The sword was not on her person when I sold her to you," her mother retorted, her fingers fumbling to undo the scabbard around Ceres's waist.

Lord Blaku growled and threw Ceres against the kitchen table so her head hit the corner, a sharp pain spreading across her temple. Lying on the floor, dizzy from the blow, Ceres heard her mother scream and furniture being thrown across the room. She opened her eyes and sat up and saw the slaver standing over her mother, slamming a chair against her mother's head.

"Ceres, help!" her mother yelled, but Ceres no longer had it in her.

Barely able to move, Ceres crawled on hands and knees toward the door. Once she had crossed the threshold, Ceres climbed onto her feet. But she had no time. She could feel Lord Blaku's arms reaching for her, his eyes burning at her back. She needed to hurry if she was to escape, but her body wouldn't move as swiftly as she told it to.

Her heart leapt in her chest when she stumbled across the front yard, and just as she reached the dirt road, she thought she was free.

Just then, Lord Blaku roared behind her. She heard the crack of a whip and then felt a thick leather cord wrap around her neck. Being tugged backward by the whip, throat strangled, blood pooling in her head, she crashed to the ground. Her hands reached for the cord, trying to loosen it, but it was secured too tightly. She knew she needed air or she would pass out, but a breath could not be drawn.

Lord Blaku picked her up, tossed her over his shoulder, and threw her into the back of the carriage. Slowly, her surroundings started to turn dark. Then darker.

In a rush, he chained her ankles and wrists, and then he loosened the whip from around her neck.

Wheezing and couching, she gasped for air, her surroundings becoming clear again, the slaver's stench oozing into her nose as she panted.

He tore the sword from around her waist and studied it for a moment.

"This is a very fine weapon indeed," he said. "Now it is mine, and I shall melt it down."

Ceres reached a hand out toward her father's sword, the chains rattling as she moved, but he slapped her hand away and hopped out of the carriage.

He headed back into the house and when he came back out, he was holding the sack of gold Ceres had left for her brothers.

The carriage bounced as he climbed onto it, and after he whipped the horses, the wheels creaked to a start. As the carriage drove off, she kept her eyes on the near black sky, watching as silhouettes of birds flew above. A tear rolled down her cheek, but she made no sound. She had no strength to cry. Now everything had been taken from her. Her money. Her sword. Her family. Her freedom.

And when she didn't show up tomorrow morning at the palace ready to work for Prince Thanos, she would have lost everything.

CHAPTER SEVEN

Miles and miles ago, Lord Blaku had unchained Ceres and had thrown her into an enclosed slave cart, and now she sat in the light of the moon, numb, beside dozens of girls in a cage wagon, bumping forward on the main road out of Delos.

The night had been freezing—it was freezing still—and with little protection from the rain, Ceres hadn't been able to sleep, shivering all the time. Cold hands gripping the bars, she huddled at the end of the moving prison on soggy straw that reeked of urine and rotting flesh. It had stopped raining about an hour ago, and now the moon and stars were out.

She had listened in on the guards' conversations, seated up above, and a few of them had mentioned something about Holheim, the capital of Northland, which, she knew, was several months' journey away. Ceres knew if she were taken there, she would have no chance of ever seeing her family or Rexus again. But she stuffed those thoughts deep down into the dead part of her heart. Glancing back, she noticed that the girl who had been coughing the entire trip had become silent and was now slouching in the rear corner, lifeless, lips blue, skin white.

A mother and two young daughters sat next to the corpse, oblivious to the girl's passing. All the daughters were focused on was competing for their mother's lap. Better they do that than be aware that death was their neighbor, Ceres thought.

A few girls seated against the wall opposite Ceres carried a look of fear in their defeated eyes, and a few others cried in silent sobs as they longingly gazed out through the cage. Ceres didn't feel fear or sadness. She couldn't allow herself to be afraid here. Someone might sense it and judge her weak, and then use her weakness against her. Instead, she numbed herself so completely, she almost didn't care what happened to her.

"Get out of my seat," a blonde girl shouted to another.

"I have been sitting here all along," the second girl replied, her skin smooth and olive in the glow of the moonlight.

The blonde pulled the olive-skinned girl up by her ears and threw her onto the sodden, straw-covered floor. A few of the girls gasped, but most looked away, pretending not to notice the ruckus.

"This is my cart," the blonde exclaimed. "All these seats are mine."

"No they aren't," a dark-skinned girl said, shooting to her feet, her hands on her hips.

48

They stared at each other for a moment, and everyone in the cart grew quiet, eyes slipping toward the rivals as they waited to see what would happen.

Hissing, the blonde shoved the dark-skinned girl, and within seconds, they were on the floor in a wrestling match, screaming at the top of their lungs as arms and legs flailed, a few eager slaves egging them on.

It was a draw. The olive-skinned girl slowly stood up and walked toward the back as her hands dappled the cage walls, blood running from her nose. The wagon hit a bump, and she wobbled as she sat down on the floor across from Ceres. Wiping the blood with her brown, threadbare, filthy sleeve, she looked Ceres in the eyes.

"I'm Anka," she said.

The moonlight shone in through the cage onto the girl's face, and Ceres thought the girl had the most peculiar eyes she had ever seen: dark brown irises with streaks of turquoise. Her hair was long, thick, and black, and Ceres guessed the girl was around her age.

"I'm Ceres."

Feeling sorry for the girl, but without any strength to become involved, Ceres looked out through the iron bars at the back of the cart, wondering if it would be possible to escape. Life as a slave was not worth living, and she'd do anything to get out, even risk her life, if it came to that.

Unexpectedly, the wagon slowed to a stop on the side of the road, as Lord Blaku yelled for his guards to break up the fight. The cart rocked as the men jumped down from the roof and into puddles of water and wet grass. His face appeared right outside the cage and Ceres heard keys rattling, his heavy breath turning into puffs of smoke.

When the door swung open, a shadow of confusion flickered across Anka's face, and when two of the five guards entered the wagon, the slaves cowered and winced. The men grabbed the wrestling girls and hauled them outside kicking and screaming.

"You're a sweet one," Lord Blaku said, grabbing Anka's arm. "Come here, girl."

Anka feverishly shook her head and scuttled backward, her eyes wide with terror, and Ceres felt a wave of nausea wash over her when she thought about what that fat, old, ugly slaver would do to the innocent girl.

Anka shrieked as Lord Blaku pulled her out.

At that moment, Ceres caught a glimpse of her sword attached around the slaver's waist, and in a split second, she saw her opportunity for escape.

Lord Blaku reached for the deadbolt, but before he could lock it, Ceres kicked the door outward and leapt out of the wagon. A few other slaves escaped and started down the street, but two guards quickly rounded up the runaways as another slammed the door to the wagon shut.

The slaver flung Anka to the ground and reached for the hilt of Ceres's sword. Ceres kneed him in the groin so he buckled forward, and before he stood up, she drew her sword and sliced his thigh, causing him to fall to the muddy road, wailing. The sword felt so light in her hand, she noticed, and the blade had cut through the slaver's thigh like butter.

Three guards threw the other slaves back into the wagon and locked it, the girls crying in disapproval.

Just as Ceres was about to pull Anka to her feet, Anka gasped and yelled, "Behind you!"

Ceres spun around to find three guards upon her. The first had his sword raised, and had Anka not warned her, Ceres would have had his blade in her back.

To her astonishment, the same power she had felt in the arena when she had saved Sartes rushed through her veins. Suddenly, she could see clearly what she needed to do in order to defeat the three guards.

She met the first guard's sword with her own several times before running her blade through him. He dropped to the side of the road in a puddle of water.

The short guard was holding a dagger, and he tossed it between his hands as he scuffled toward her. She kept her eye on the dagger for a few switches, and timing it just right, she flicked her sword between his hands so the dagger went flying into the air, landing on top of the slaver wagon.

"Let me go and I will let you live," Ceres said, so much authority in her voice, not even she recognized it.

"Anyone who captures her will receive fifty-five pieces of gold!" Lord Blaku yelled, throwing his whip toward the short guard who lost his dagger.

Ha! My mother's gold, Ceres thought, adding to her anger.

The two remaining guards inched toward her, the tall one with a patch over his eye drawing his sword, the short one cracking the whip. At the palace, Ceres had only ever fought one on one with others, and she felt uneasy having to conquer two at the same time. But then again, there, she hadn't been fighting for her life, and she hadn't felt that overwhelming surge of force she was feeling now.

The short man snapped the whip so it latched around Ceres's sword hand, and with a tug, Ceres fell to the ground, face first. She had gripped her sword so hard that it still remained in her hand, and with one hack, she severed the leather cords from around her wrist, freeing herself.

Quick as a cat, she sprung to her feet, and just as tall guard attacked, she lunged toward him, their swords colliding.

The short guard threw himself toward Ceres and wrapped arms around her legs so she couldn't move, causing her to topple over, crashing onto her back. He crawled on top of her and wrapped one hand around her sword arm, confining it, the other around her neck, choking her.

"Kill her if you must!" Lord Blaku shouted, still holding his hands around his bleeding thigh.

Ceres kicked her feet up and knocked the short guard in the head, shoving him off her as she rolled backward and up to a standing position. Seeing he was about to stagger to his feet, Ceres kicked him in the face several times until he slumped to the ground unconscious.

Just as the tall guard came at her, she swerved around him, struck his feet from under him, and once he had fallen onto his back, she sliced off his hand. He screamed as blood oozed from his stub.

She hadn't meant to be so brutal. She only wanted to harm him enough so he couldn't fight anymore and wouldn't follow her when she ran away, but the blade was exceptionally sharp and it took almost no effort to slash through his bones. Or perhaps it was this strange force that made it so effortless?

Some of girls in the wagon had climbed up the sides of the wall, rattling the cage, screaming for Ceres to let them out. Others cheered Ceres on, chanting for her to kill their captors.

"Give up your sword, or the girl dies," Lord Blaku yelled behind her.

Ceres whirled around to see Anka held at knifepoint by the slaver. Anka's bottom lip trembled, her eyes wide open, and the slaver pressed the blade into her throat, cutting her a little.

Should she try and save Anka? Ceres could just make a run for it and she would be free. But Anka's eyes pleaded with such desperation that Ceres couldn't find it in her heart to leave her to such a horrid fate. She glanced over at the girls in the wagon, who had turned quiet, realizing she could free them, too.

Ceres leaned back and threw her sword, praying her aim was true.

She watched as it spun end over end, then finally landed in Lord Blaku's face, the blade stabbing him in the eye. He fell backwards, landing flat in the mud.

Dead.

With a whimper, Anka crawled away from him, sobbing.

Ceres, breathing hard, walked forward in the quiet, pulled her sword out from the slaver's skull, and then walked over and slashed the lock off the wagon, opening the door. Shouting and sighing in delight, the women and girls streamed out of the cart one after another. A few thanked Ceres as they passed her, and the mother with her daughters embraced Ceres before turning back toward Delos.

With arms and legs feeling like they weighed a hundred pounds each, and her eyes heavy from sleeplessness, Ceres walked to the front of the wagon and cut the reins to the horses. She took a blanket, a bag of food, and a leather flask filled with wine from atop the wagon and attached it to one of the horses.

After she had removed the scabbard from Lord Blaku's carcass and secured her sword around her waist, she mounted the stout brown mare and steered it southward toward Delos. Just as she passed Anka, she stopped.

"You saved my life," Anka said. "I am indebted to you."

"You saved me first," Ceres replied. "You owe me nothing."

"Let me join you. Please. I have nowhere to go."

Ceres considered Anka's suggestion and thought it might be nice to have company on the cold, dark road back.

"Very well, Anka. We shall travel together," Ceres said with a soft smile.

She reached out her hand and pulled Anka up behind her, Anka clinging to Ceres's back as if for dear life. As lightning struck in the distance, the clouds rolling in again, Ceres prodded the horse to gallop. She would have time to spare before she needed to be at the palace, and she knew where she needed to go: to Rexus and her brothers.

CHAPTER EIGHT

The night remained brutally cold, the wind a roaring tempest, but that didn't prevent Ceres from compelling the horse forward at a furious pace, determined to reach Rexus if there was enough time. For hours, rain whipped against her like shards of ice, leaving her clothes sopping wet and her fingers frozen stiff, anger toward her mother and Lord Blaku driving her.

Finally, she sighted the capital's outer wall, and, as the rain ended, she slowed the horse to a trot. The sun crested the Alva Mountains, sparkling through dissipating clouds, and kissed the white buildings of the capital golden, and with about an hour to spare until she needed to be at the palace, Ceres hopped down from the horse and led the mare down the gently sloping gorge to the river. After she had escorted the horse to water, she unwrapped the bread and meat she had taken from Lord Blaku and portioned equal parts for Anka and herself.

She sat down on a rock and glanced at Anka, who was scarfing down the food like a ravenous animal.

"Would you like for me to take you home?" she asked Anka.

Anka paused and looked up, her eyes suddenly weary, but she said nothing.

"Perhaps now that the slaver is dead, your family—"

"My parents sold me to save their farm. Twenty pieces of gold," Anka said bitterly. "They are no longer my family."

Ceres understood. Oh, how she understood. She looked toward the Alva Mountains and thought for a moment.

"I know where you might find a new home," she said.

"Where?" Anka asked, taking a sip of the wine.

"My brothers and friends are part of the revolution."

Anka squinted her eyes, and then she nodded.

"You are my sister now and they shall be my family and friends. I shall fight by your side and belong to the revolution, too," she said.

Once they finished their meal, Ceres led the mare back onto the road and rode with Anka down the sloping hillside toward the capital's main entrance—a heavily guarded drawbridge made of thick oak. Getting in line behind other travelers and merchants, Ceres and Anka rode slowly past a soldier and onto the bridge.

They rode through the cobblestone streets, past houses and wooden shacks, and down cramped alleyways. The city began to rise, the inhabitants lining up at the living wells with buckets and vessels. Children played in the streets, their laughter filling the air, reminding Ceres of much happier, much simpler times.

Beyond acres and acres of wilted, brown plants, they arrived at the bottom of the Alva Mountains. Humble houses rested on the gently sloping hill, sheltered by jutting peaks, and a waterfall cascaded down the mountainside. From the outside, the small settlement looked like any ordinary one on the outskirts of Delos, with houses, wagons, animals, and peasants working the fields. But it was nothing but a façade to keep Empire soldiers from growing suspicious. Inside every abode, a rebellion was brewing.

Ceres had been here once before: two years ago when Rexus had shown her the growing collection of weapons stored in the cave behind the waterfall.

Outside the settlement, bordering on the sea, stood the old abandoned castle: the revolution's headquarters. Two of three towers had collapsed, and a few of the walls had been patched up with driftwood and rocks. Ceres's destination.

They dismounted and walked down the sandy pathway, the breeze from the sea tugging on Ceres's clothes. Once they arrived at the arching entryway, five heavily armored men wearing civilian clothes stopped them.

"My name is Ceres. I am here for Rexus, my friend, and Nesos and Sartes, my brothers," she said, staying the horse. "This is Anka, my friend. We want to join the rebellion."

One of the men's eyes flared a tad, as if her name held some significance. He nodded and headed into the courtyard while the other men studied the girls with distrustful glances.

Inside the courtyard, Ceres could see men and women working in a rushed, almost frantic manner. Some were training others in sword fighting; some were fashioning armor; some were making bows and whittling sticks into arrows; and yet others were sewing clothes.

A few minutes passed, and then a few more. Were Rexus and her brothers not here? Ceres wondered. Would she have to leave without seeing them? She had to see them before she left for the palace.

All of a sudden, Rexus burst around the corner.

"Ciri!" he yelled, running toward her.

Seeing his face again, Ceres felt her strength leave her, and when he wrapped eager arms around her, she broke down and sobbed. She had been strong for so long, and now standing wrapped in his safe embrace, she finally let her weakness surface.

"I thought you were dead," he said, stroking her back, squeezing her tight.

He rained kisses on her face, drying up her tears, and then he pressed his soft warm mouth to hers. But his lips were gone even before she had a chance to enjoy their first kiss.

"I was worried sick about you," he said, clutching her tightly. "Sartes said he saw you outside your father's shed, but that you vanished after that."

"Are my brothers here?" she asked.

"Not at the moment," Rexus replied. 'They are on an assignment."

Ceres felt her heart sink, but she nodded and took a step back.

"This is my friend Anka," she said, placing a hand on her new friend's shoulder. "She was also in the slaver wagon. She needs a place to stay."

"In a slaver wagon? That's why you look the way you do," Rexus said, playful eyes running up and down her body.

Ceres socked him in the shoulder.

"You certainly don't look any better than me," she said with a smirk, causing Rexus to laugh.

"Please get Fausta for me," Rexus said to a guard. He turned to Ceres, a conflicted look on his face. "Are you not staying?"

Ceres was torn. Part of her wanted to stay here with Rexus and her brothers, but a huge part of her wanted to work as a weapon-keeper.

"I have been hired by Prince Thanos as his weapon-keeper."

Rexus's eyes flared, and then he nodded.

An elderly woman waddled toward them with the guard, her crinkly skin white as snow, her eyes filled with years of suffering and wisdom.

"Fausta," Rexus said. "Please see to it that Anka is given a place to stay. And make sure she has food and dry clothes."

The old woman opened her frail arms and embraced the newcomer.

"You have a new home now, and we will see each other often," Ceres said to Anka. "I owe you my life and I shall never forget you."

Anka smiled softly and nodded. She gave Ceres a hug, and then she followed Fausta into the courtyard.

Taking Ceres's hand in his, Rexus grabbed the horse's reins and escorted them toward the stable. Once there, he let go of Ceres and led the horse to the water trough.

"You have a new sword," he said, not looking back, stroking the horse's mane.

The mare whinnied in approval.

"Yes. A gift from my father," she said, her hand automatically feeling for it, a pang of sadness overwhelming her.

But she didn't want to talk about sad things.

"The rebellion seems to have grown," she said.

"Since I last brought you here, our supporters have tripled in number," he said.

It made Ceres happy to see wonderment in his eyes.

They walked outside and sat down on a wooden bench, Rexus facing her. He gently stroked her hair, and then caressed her face.

A void opened within her chest when she thought of saying good-bye, and again she entertained the idea of remaining here.

"Perhaps I will stay with you," she said.

Rexus pressed his lips together.

"I would love that, but I think the best thing is if you keep your appointment at the palace," he said.

Ceres knew he was right, but still, it hurt to hear him say she should go.

"Here, we have many supporters," Rexus continued. "But we have no one working within the palace walls."

"I don't know how much access I would have to the inside or the other royals," she said.

"If you gain Prince Thanos's trust, I'm certain he would give you access to all the rebellion needs. When the moment is right, you could lead us inside the palace, securing our victory," he said.

Ceres's stomach churned at the thought of gaining Prince Thanos's trust only to betray him. But why? Perhaps it was because he did trust her and had given her a chance where others would not. Or perhaps it was because he despised his family and what they stood for just as much as any commoner.

Either way, Rexus was right: by doing this, she could help the rebellion like no one else. In fact, her presence inside the castle walls was just what the rebellion needed, and could very well play a significant part in the downfall of the Empire.

She nodded, and for a brief moment, they held each other's eyes.

Not wanting to drag out the farewell, the sadness already overwhelming her, Ceres rose to her feet and walked into the barn. Just as she was about to mount the horse, she heard Rexus enter behind her. While securing the saddle, she glanced back.

"I must go so I am not late for the palace. Please take care of my brothers, and Anka," she said.

Rexus placed a hand on her shoulder and tingles spread through Ceres's body. Ceres thought about the kiss they had shared earlier. Had he meant to kiss her as a friend, or something more? She wanted it to be more. She knew if she turned around, she would find his eyes and his lips would meet hers. And then she wouldn't be able to tear herself away.

So without another word she mounted her horse and kicked, galloping away, far from this place, and toward the palace—determined not to look back for anything.

CHAPTER NINE

As the sun broke over the horizon and with hardly a second to spare, Ceres galloped through the palace gates, dropped off the horse at the royal stables, and darted toward the palace training ground. When she was almost halfway, she noticed her sword brushing against her leg, and she stopped. Would someone see her sword and perhaps even steal it from her if she brought it? She knew there was no time, and she could be fired for being late, but under no circumstances could she afford to lose this sword.

As fast as her feet could carry her, she sprinted back to the blacksmith's chalet, and finding the place empty, she climbed up the ladder to the loft. There, behind a pile of old planks and crooked twigs, she hid her sword before tearing toward the palace training ground.

When she arrived—breathless, heart thumping wildly— to her surprise, she saw that the entire court had gathered around the practice arena. The king and queen sat on their thrones, princes and princesses on chairs beneath the willow trees, fanning themselves, and the advisors and dignitaries sat on benches, whispering to each other.

In the practice arena, combatlords sparred against royals, and weapon-keepers were watching their masters, handing off swords, daggers, tridents, shields, and floggers. Since she could remember, Ceres had yearned for an opportunity like this, but now that the moment was here, she felt empty inside.

"Ceres!" Thanos yelled, waving to her.

She didn't know why, but when she saw him again, her heart stirred. Then she reprimanded herself. She had to remember why she was here, which was to befriend her enemies and gain their trust, not be amused by a handsome prince who somehow seemed to put her under his spell.

Ceres ran over to Thanos.

"Right on time," he said with a nod.

"Of course," she said as if getting here hadn't been a miracle and a half.

An Empire soldier marched to the center of the arena.

"All royal warriors, hastily line up before King Claudius, your weapon-keepers behind you," he said.

The royals stopped what they were doing and Ceres followed Thanos, taking her place behind him. She noticed that Lucious was back. Had he reconsidered? Been forced to return?

"You're wondering about Lucious?" Thanos asked, glancing back at her.

"Yes."

Ceres wasn't sure whether she hated it or liked it that he was so in tune with her thoughts.

"One doesn't say no to the king," Thanos whispered.

She wanted to ask why, but the king rose, holding a golden bowl up, and the gathering hushed.

"This dish is filled with the names of each of our royal warriors," the king said. "Today I will select three names who will fight in the Killings at noon."

The crowd gasped, each royal warrior and their weapon-keepers included.

But the Killings weren't supposed to be until next month, Ceres thought. Had the king just on a whim scheduled the Killings for today?

She glanced at Thanos, but he stood rigid as a board, his face forward so she couldn't see his expression. They weren't ready to fight in the Killings, Ceres knew. None of them were. They hadn't been given enough time to train together, to get to know each other's fighting styles.

Winding her hands tightly into fists, she focused on keeping her breathing steady. Only three of twelve would be selected, so there was still a chance they didn't have to fight today.

The king reached his chubby hand into the bowl and pulled out a slip.

"Lucious!" he yelled, an evil grin emerging on his lips.

Ceres exhaled and glanced over at Lucious, seeing that his face had turned as red as a beet. The onlookers clapped, although their applause was far from enthusiastic. Did they think this was unfair, too? Ceres wondered.

The king reached into the bowl again and drew a name.

"Georgio!" he hollered, his eyes slithering to the end of the line where Georgio waited.

A woman who looked old enough to be Georgio's mother stood up began to sob, yelling obscenities toward the king, but when she stepped onto the practice arena, she was escorted away by Empire soldiers.

Ceres huffed and kept her eyes trained on Thanos's broad back. Only one name left, she told herself. The chances of Thanos being selected were slim.

Reaching his hand into the bowl a third time, the king glanced at Thanos and the right side of his lip rose.

Ceres saw Thanos's shoulders tense, and immediately she knew something wasn't quite right. Had the king planned this? Rigged this?

Her heart nearly stopped.

"And last but not least, Thanos!" the king exclaimed with a smug smile.

The crowd went silent for a moment, but when the queen started to applaud with fervent enthusiasm, the others followed.

"The risk of death is great, my chosen ones. May you each represent your sovereign and Empire with honor and strength," the king continued.

The king sat down and an Empire soldier explained the rules of the Killings, but Ceres could hardly listen to a word he said, she was so shocked.

"Weapon-keepers who assist in the battle will be put to death...no more than three weapons on any one warrior at one time...no helping other combatlords...thumbs-up means the defeated lives, thumbs-down means the defeated must be slayed..." the Empire soldier said.

When he finished, Ceres stood frozen, staring out into thin air.

She vaguely registered that Thanos had turned around and was facing her. He grabbed her arm and shook it.

"Ceres!" he said.

Disoriented, she looked up into his face.

"Bartholomew is back. If you would like, I can have him be my weapon-keeper today," Thanos said.

At first, her heart leapt in her chest and she wanted to shout yes. Yes! But then she thought of the conversation she had had with Rexus. How would she earn Thanos's trust if she backed out now? She wouldn't.

"Is that what you want?" she asked.

"I prefer to work with you, but seeing the rules have changed, I will not hold it against you if you decide to sit this round out," he said.

She couldn't believe it. Here he was giving her freedom, and she was scheming how to best earn his trust so she could destroy him and his family. A feeling of guilt began to take root.

But then she remembered her people's suffering: the young boy who had been whipped in Fountain Square and hauled off to an unknown destination, the girl who had died in the slaver wagon alone and afraid, her brothers who never went to bed with full bellies, and her father who had to leave his family to make money elsewhere.

If she didn't stand up for them, who would?

"Then I will be your weapon-keeper today and for as long as you would have me," Ceres said.

Thanos nodded, and a hint of a smile graced his lips.

"We shall conquer together," he said.

*

With sweaty hands and an unsettled stomach, Ceres peered down the tunnel underneath the Stade. The passageway was crawling with Empire soldiers, combatlords, and weapon-keepers, weapons of every kind lining the walls, strewn across the gravel floors.

She sat down on a bench mere feet away from the iron gates, waiting for her and Thanos's turn, the crowd chanting like a dragon outside.

"Kill him! Kill him! Kill him!" they shouted.

The onlookers roared, and not a minute later, the iron gates opened, chains clattering, and in strode two Empire soldiers, each hauling mutilated, dead combatlords. They threw one corpse on top of the other onto the dirt floor right across from where Ceres sat, and then they darted back out into the arena.

Ceres startled when the iron gate slammed shut behind them, and she couldn't help but slide her eyes toward the lifeless bodies. Just minutes ago, those men had stood in front of her full of vigor, certain they would be triumphant in today's competition. Now they rested in a heap on the floor, never to rise again.

When she glanced up at Thanos, his eyes were already on her, those impossibly dark irises carrying solemnity that Ceres had only ever seen in the dying. Was he afraid like she was? she wondered.

She watched as he tightened the thick leather belt around his canvas loincloth, his rigid abdomen exposed. She could hardly believe what little protection he wore: a single leather shoulder guard covering his right arm. Most of the other warriors hid behind heavy armor and shining helmets.

Ceres had been given a uniform: a blue short-sleeved tunic that reached to her knees, a silk rope around her waist, and soft leather knee-high boots that resembled Thanos's. Although she didn't particularly like it, she was glad to be out of her old clothes that did nothing but remind her of her old life.

"Did the king set you up?" Ceres asked, remembering King Claudius's sly expression when he hand-picked the royal warriors' names from the golden bowl.

"Yes," Thanos said.

She clenched her teeth and a fire of hate burned within.

"This isn't right," she said.

"No, it isn't," Thanos said, sitting down beside her, tightening the straps on his boots. "But if there is one thing I have learned, it is that you don't refuse the king."

"Have you refused him before?" she asked.

He nodded.

"For what?"

"I wouldn't marry the princess he had chosen for me."

She stared at him for a moment, stunned. She was amazed at the courage that must have taken. Perhaps the girl was hideous, although Ceres hadn't seen any hideous princesses her entire life, all of them dressed in fine clothing, bathed in sweet-smelling perfumes, and adorned with exquisite jewelry.

She looked away, wondering who this young man really was. A rebel? Ceres had not once considered that there might be a nonconformist within the palace walls.

She had a whole new respect for Thanos. Perhaps he was not the boy she thought he was. Which made her feel even sicker to betray him.

"And what of Lucious and Georgio?" she asked.

"The king despises them for other reasons."

"But how can the king can just randomly—"

He interrupted her, his voice impatient.

"Just because I am royalty doesn't mean I have a say in my life."

Ceres hadn't thought about that. She had always assumed the royals were free to do as they pleased and that they ruled as one big enemy.

"All the pomp and haughtiness, the rules, decorum, frivolous spending…it drives me to the brink of insanity," he said, almost growling.

Ceres was taken aback that he would say such things about the royals and didn't know exactly what to say to him. Instead, she looked out the iron gates, and just as she did, she saw a combatlord stab Georgio's weapon-keeper through the abdomen.

Her hand hit her mouth and she gasped.

In her naiveté, she had assumed she was safe from other combatlords since she wasn't the one fighting. A sense of dread gripped her shoulders and she noticed how her hands shook even more than before.

An Empire soldier approached, telling Thanos it was his turn to fight next, and that he would be fighting together with Lucious against two other combatlords.

With a parched throat, Ceres said, "We have to stick together if we are to make it out alive."

Thanos nodded, a quiet understanding between them.

They stood up and walked over to the iron gates, each in their own thoughts for some time.

"I won't kill unless I have to," Thanos suddenly said.

Ceres nodded, wondering if this was one more way he planned to defy the king.

"I need to know I can trust you with my life," he said without looking away from the arena.

"You can trust me with your life," Ceres said, wondering if he heard the slight hesitation in her voice.

He closed his eyes and nodded.

"You can trust me with your life, too, Ceres," he said.

She didn't know why, but his words sank into her bones, and she felt they were true. Despite herself, she was feeling an intense bond with him.

Lucious and his weapon-keeper stepped up behind Thanos and Ceres, and Ceres noticed Lucious's shiny full body armor and visored helmet. No amount of armor will save a sloppy warrior's life, she thought.

The iron gates swung open, and in came Georgio alive, his body drenched in sweat, blood dripping from a few lacerations to his arms and abdomen. An Empire soldier dragged his weapon-keeper in behind him and flung him on top of the other cadavers on the floor.

Ceres's entire body started to shake.

"Stay close to me," Thanos said, his eyes straight forward as if in a trance, his jaw clenching.

Just as the Empire soldier nodded for them to exit, Lucious shoved Ceres out of the way and entered the arena first, his arms held high in the air as if in victory. The masses went wild, and he paraded around for a few moments, reveling in their approval.

At any other time than this very moment, his behavior would have irritated Ceres to no end, but standing here, inhaling what could quite possibly be her last breath, she paid no attention to the approval-seeking fool.

Thanos and Ceres entered the arena next, and Ceres squinted, the sun blinding her. Once her eyes had adjusted to the light, she glanced up into the audience, seeing only roughly half the seats filled.

She gazed up at the podium and saw the king sitting up on his throne, smiling glumly. How she despised him. If what Thanos said was true, he was eviler than Ceres had imagined.

"Remember, stay close," Thanos said, touching her elbow.

She nodded and then spotted the two combatlords on the other side of the arena, wearing heavy armor, each holding a sword.

When the trumpets blared, at once, a beast sprung out from one of the trap doors in the ground. It charged toward Ceres and Thanos, its grizzled black fur glistening in the sunlight, its roar echoing against the stadium walls. The dog-like creature was unfamiliar to Ceres—large body, stalky legs—and moved at a slower pace compared to an omnicat, although she didn't doubt it was just as strong.

"A wolver!" someone from the crowd yelled, and then a wave of clamors moved through the audience.

Adrenaline coursed through her, and for a moment, she didn't know where to go. But when she saw the weapons lined up against the wall, she headed toward them and waited for Thanos's command.

First, Thanos called for the trident, and she flung it to him. Good choice, she thought as she watched him catch it mid-air. She wanted to jump in and help him, but she remembered the rule forbidding a weapon-keeper to intervene.

Thanos screamed at the wolver as he jabbed the trident toward the beast, his feet moving with swiftness, his reflexes lightning quick.

From the corner of her eye, Ceres noticed one of the combatlords making his way toward Thanos. If he were smart, the combatlord would wait to strike until after Thanos had slain the wolver or the beast might attack him, too.

All of a sudden, the wolver charged toward Thanos, and Thanos jabbed it in the shoulder. The onlookers cheered in approval at the fight's first attack.

However, the wolver didn't seem to be injured in the least, only growling louder from what Thanos had done, licking its teeth, red eyes glaring at Thanos.

"Longsword!" Thanos yelled.

Right as she threw it to him, he dropped the trident to the ground and caught the longsword mid-air. But then suddenly, Ceres sensed he needed protection from fire— quick—and she yelled at him and also threw him a shield. Just as he caught the shield, the

64

wolver inhaled, and then it spewed fire from its mouth. The onlookers gasped, and Thanos ducked behind the shield, the flames blasting against the metal surface.

Once the wolver had run out of breath, Thanos dropped his shield, picked up the trident, and hurled it at the beast's head, piercing its eye.

The animal violently shook its head as it snarled and growled, sending the trident flying halfway across the arena, Ceres saw.

Without hesitating, Thanos tore toward the wolver, leapt into the air, and lifted his sword. On his way down, he stabbed the beast in the head, and it fell lifeless onto the red sand.

But even though the audience cheered, there was no rest. The combatlord that had been lying in wait charged, his spear and sword pointed straight at Thanos.

Thanos pulled and pulled, trying to dislodge the blade from the wolver's skull, Ceres saw. But it wouldn't budge. And he already had three weapons on the field; the trident on the other side of the arena, his shield too far to reach, and the blade wedged into the wolver's skull. Ceres knew it was against the rules to throw him another one.

She held her breath. The combatlord was close. Too close. She stepped forward.

Still pulling on the blade, Thanos looked at Ceres, his eyes wide with fear, his face twisted in desperation.

He was going to die.

And there was nothing Ceres could do to prevent it.

CHAPTER TEN

Screaming, Thanos desperately tugged at the blade lodged in the wolver's skull, but even as fiercely as he tried, the sword would not budge in the least. Hearing the combatlord's footsteps approaching, he glanced back to see his enemy a mere ten feet away. His life depended on retrieving his sword, for he knew a weaponless warrior was a dead warrior.

Fraught, he looked to Ceres, but he knew three weapons were on the field and if she threw him another one, she would be punished.

She raised a palm toward him, and just as he heard the swooshing sound of his opponent's blade descending, Thanos's sword jutted into his hand as if by some mystical force.

Shocked at what happened but with no time to linger on it, Thanos spun and rolled on the ground, the combatlord's sword just missing him by a fraction of an inch, the crowd's roar peaking into a frenzy before retreating into a static hum.

Thanos was quick to hop to his feet, and just then, he heard Lucious calling for help. Seeing his opponent several feet away, Thanos afforded a quick glance and discovered Lucious stripped of a weapon, his weapon-keeper lying facedown in the red sand.

"Throw me something! Anything!" Lucious yelled to Ceres, his voice filled with rage. "Do it now or I'll have you skinned alive!"

As Thanos snapped his attention back towards his foe, he vaguely registered that Ceres tossed Lucious two daggers. But his irritation was replaced with alarm when he saw the combatlord hurling a spear at him.

Just as the spear approached, Thanos clenched a fist around it, stopping it from penetrating his heart, and then he whirled the spear around and flung it back at the combatlord, piercing his thigh exactly where he had meant to.

"Thanos! Thanos! Thanos!" the audience shouted, fists pumping into the air.

The combatlord fell to his feet, moaning in pain, holding his leg, the spear protruding from it.

Recognizing his opportunity, Thanos ran behind the combatlord and hit him on the head with the hilt of his sword, knocking him unconscious.

However, even before he could look to the king for acceptance of his victory, Lucious encircled him—and suddenly Lucious's combatlord attacked Thanos, forcing Thanos to continue fighting.

The scoundrel pawned his combatlord onto me, Thanos thought.

It was as he had always suspected: Lucious had absolutely no honor.

While he was battling a new opponent, Thanos could see Lucious sauntering over to the iron gate.

"Let me in or I will kill you and find your family and torture them all to death!" Lucious yelled.

Thanos heard the gate rattling as it opened, the crowed booing Lucious.

"Thanos!" Ceres yelled, holding up two daggers.

Of course. He was growing weary and needed lighter weapons. He nodded toward her, and she threw them to him.

Right away, Thanos kicked the combatlord in the chest so he flew backward. But with impeccable balance, the combatlord landed on his feet and charged toward Thanos, sword in hand. The combatlord lunged forward, thrusting his sword toward Thanos, but Thanos jumped out of the way.

As they moved around the arena, Thanos noticed that little by little, his nemesis grew exhausted, his chest heaving greatly with each breath, his movements slackening a hair. His plan was working. He didn't want to kill the man, no, only exhaust him so he could render him unconscious like he had the first one.

Right as Thanos approached his shield, he picked it up from the ground and flung it into the combatlord's face. The combatlord fell to the ground lifeless, and for the first time since he could remember since entering the arena, the spectators went silent.

Thanos panted and gazed up at the podium, awaiting the king's decision, hoping he would not be commanded to murder his unconscious adversary.

However, from what he knew about the blood-thirsty monarch, Thanos feared King Claudius would force him to do something he had worked hard to avoid—kill.

The king glowered at Thanos as if he didn't accept that the battle had ended in Thanos's favor, the tension between the two palpable, the entire Stade void of the faintest of sounds. After arising from his seat, the king walked to the edge of the platform, his hand outstretched, his thumb outstretched to the side.

Finally, the king lifted a thumb up with a frown, and the onlookers broke into applause.

Thanos couldn't believe it. Ceres and he had survived. They had survived!

He looked over at Ceres, feeling drops of sweat dripping from his hair and down his face. He nodded, and when she smiled, it was as if in that instance, the victory was complete.

He stared at her, stunned. She had saved his life more than once, and had done it in a way he did not understand.

And for the first time since he'd met her, he was beginning to wonder.

Who was she?

CHAPTER ELEVEN

A tear rolled down Ceres's cheek as her fingers carefully skimmed the weapons laid out on tables in the practice arena. Amidst the twilight she heard laughter and music spilling out from the open palace windows, every royal inside those haughty walls celebrating today's great victories. It made her feel more alone than ever. It made her miss her brothers, her father, her home, Rexus, dearly. It made her mourn for the mother she'd never had.

Ceres paused and listened to the wind sighing through the trees, as she looked up and saw a few stars twinkling down on her. She inhaled the fresh air, the scent of roses and lilies filling her nostrils. The quiet was a welcome friend after the roaring crowd at the Stade. Even if she had been invited to the feast, she wouldn't have wanted to accept, having no desire to mingle with those pompous royals who were congratulating each other for a battle Thanos and she had won.

Thanos. Her insides coiled tightly when she thought of how he hadn't even bothered to see her after the Killings. There was no "thank you." No "job well done." But she didn't need his approval or his praise, she reminded herself. She didn't need anyone.

Upset with herself for allowing such ludicrous melancholy, she wiped the tears from her cheeks, picked up a spear, and walked to the center of the practice arena.

Swinging the spear overhead, she whirled it around until a swooshing sound could be heard. She then hurled it at a training dummy, hitting it right on the center of the smallest circle. She smiled.

Feeling much lighter, she meandered over to the table again and picked out a sword—one that reminded her of her own, its blade thin and long, its hilt bronze and gold.

Lunging forward, she pretended to attack Lucious—the coward—her sword moving with deftness, her attention and anger on her imaginary enemy.

Keep light afoot. She jumped. *Attack and defend.* She lunged. *Be fluid like water, strong like a mountain.* It was what her trainers at the palace had pounded into her. And it was what she had practiced for hours and months and years.

"After today, I would have thought you'd be tucked in bed, falling fast asleep."

She turned with a start to find Thanos stepping out from behind a willow tree, smiling.

69

Ceres lowered her sword and turned toward him, her cheeks hot with embarrassment. She saw he wore a loose linen shirt, the neck open, and dark curls framed his face. She tried to hate him in this moment.

But somehow her heart had warmed with his presence.

"I could say the same to you," she said, raising an eyebrow, hoping he wouldn't notice her racing heart.

"I was about to—but then I heard someone practicing in the arena below my room."

She looked up the tower to the balcony, his door open, red curtains dancing in the wind.

"I'm sorry I kept you up, my lord," she said, looking back at him.

"Thanos, please," he said, bowing toward her, keeping eye contact.

He smiled and took a step toward her.

"You weren't really keeping me up. I left the party as soon as I could to look for you, and that's when I saw you from my balcony," he said.

"Why were you looking for me?" she asked, trying to ignore the nervous energy that pulsed through her.

"I wanted to thank you for today," he said.

She stared at him blankly for a moment, trying to hold onto the anger for him that was quickly vanishing.

"What brilliant skill you have," he said. "You have been taught well."

She wouldn't reveal she had been dressing up as a boy, training with the combatlords at the palace. He could report her. And he would, wouldn't he? They might be allies in the arena, but in the real world, they were enemies.

"My father was a bladesmith," she said, hoping he wouldn't pry anymore into her training.

He nodded.

"And where is he now?" Thanos asked.

Ceres looked down, thoughts of her father hundreds of miles away weighing heavily on her mind.

"He had to take work elsewhere," she whispered.

"I'm sad to hear, Ceres," Thanos said, stepping even closer.

She wished he would stay away, for when he was this close, it was hard to consider him her nemesis and to despise him so.

"And what of your mother?" he asked, watching her closely.

"She tried to sell me into slavery," Ceres admitted, thinking there was no harm in telling him the truth about her mother.

70

He nodded once, and squeezed his lips together.

"I'm sorry," he said.

It irritated her that he apologized for that. A prince. It was partly his fault her father hadn't been paid enough at the palace and needed to look for work elsewhere.

"How are your wounds?" she asked, walking over to the table and placing the sword on it, hoping to steer the conversation onto safer subjects.

"They'll heal," he said as he followed after her.

Standing next to her, his arms folded, he studied her face for a moment.

"How did you do that?" he asked.

"What?" Ceres said.

"Out in the arena today. First, you threw me a shield. I have never heard of a wolver, let alone that any animal could spew flames."

She shrugged her shoulders.

"I had heard of wolvers from my father," she fibbed.

"Then, my sword…it was lodged in the wolver's skull," he said, his eyes squinting. "You raised your hand and the blade jutted into my hand with this force—"

"I did no such thing!" Ceres interrupted him, backing away, afraid he was onto her.

He glanced at her with kind eyes and cocked his head to the side.

"Are you saying I imagined it?" he asked.

She balked. Was he trying to trap her? She needed to choose her words carefully or she could be thrown into prison for implying he was a liar.

"I am certain I don't know what you are talking about," she said.

His eyebrows knitted together and he opened his mouth as if to speak, but instead, he stepped toward her, placed a hand on her shoulder, and let it slide down her arm.

A delightful shiver went through Ceres, and she loathed how her body betrayed her so.

"No matter," he said. "Thank you, though. Your selections of weapons made all the difference."

"Yes, perhaps your lovely hair would have been singed off had I not offered the shield," she said with a smirk, trying to make light of the situation.

"You think I have lovely hair?" he asked.

71

Her breathing staggered, and she couldn't understand how she could have let such a flippant comment escape her lips.

"No," she said rather sharply, folding her arms in front of her chest.

His lips twitched.

"Well, then, I don't think you have beautiful eyes, either," he said.

"Then it's settled."

He nodded and Ceres walked over to a willow tree.

"It's getting late," she said.

"Perhaps I may escort you home?" he said, following her again.

Ceres lowered her gaze and shook her head.

"Or perhaps you need a place to stay?" he asked, his voice barely above a whisper.

Should she tell him the truth? If she didn't, she knew she would have to sleep outdoors every night.

"Yes," she said.

"There is no room for you inside the castle walls, but just down that path next to the well is a vacant summer home, and you are welcome to stay there."

He pointed to a small cottage secluded by trees, covered in vines.

"I would be very grateful," she said.

He took her arm and was about to walk her there, but then a girl emerged from the bushes. She was lovely, Ceres thought, with blonde hair and brown eyes, her skin as smooth as silk, her lips blood red. She wore a white silk dress, and when a breeze gusted against Ceres's face, she noticed the girl smelled of roses.

Feeling a bit awkward, Ceres pulled her arm away from Thanos's.

"Hello, Stephania," Thanos said, and Ceres could detect a slight irritation in his voice.

Stephania smiled at Thanos, but when her eyes reached Ceres, the girl frowned.

"Whom have we here?" Stephania asked.

"This is Ceres, my weapon-keeper," Thanos said.

"Where are you going with your weapon-keeper?" Stephania asked.

"That is none of your concern," Thanos replied.

"I am certain King Claudius would be thrilled to know you are meeting with your female weapon-keeper late at night, escorting her to unknown destinations," Stephania said.

"I'm certain the king would be equally thrilled to learn you are wandering around the palace grounds late at night in your sleepwear, unescorted by your handmaidens," Thanos snapped.

Stephania lifted her nose up, turned on her heels, and vanished down the paved walkway and back into the palace.

"Never mind her," Thanos said. "She's just upset I refused to marry her."

"It was her?" Ceres asked.

He didn't respond to her question, just jutted out his elbow, offering it to her again.

"Perhaps she was right. Maybe this is inappropriate," Ceres said.

"Nonsense," he said, and then he paused before smirking and saying, "Unless you were considering making it so?"

"Of course not," Ceres said, bothered, her cheeks flushing hot.

When she looped an arm through his to prove her point, she became irritated with herself for liking it, and immediately, she strengthened her resolve to not let the charming prince anywhere near her heart.

CHAPTER TWELVE

Standing atop a hill overlooking Cumorla, the capital of Haylon, a remote isle in the Mazeronian Sea, Commander Akila's heart soared with joy as he watched the statue of King Claudius come tumbling down. He inhaled the air, and the sweet sensation of justice filled him, as smoke from the king's castle rose into the azure heaven above the city.

Justice, Akila thought. Justice was finally being served today. Every last royal relative of the king had been locked inside that abominable seven-spired structure, and now it had burned down.

Wind pushed at his armor as he beheld the thousands of men on the hillside, their red banners flapping for the revolution's cause. Before twilight, he would lead them into a battle that would free them, finally, from centuries of oppression. His chest swelled with pride.

The people of Haylon had suffered long enough under the rule of tyrannical kings. They had paid unreasonable taxes, sent their best warriors to Delos, and bowed their heads to the ten thousand Empire soldiers that plagued the streets day and night. His entire life, Akila had watched women and daughters raped, children flogged and arrested. The young were forced to work long days in the king's fields, returning with welts and dejected eyes. He knew it was long past since they needed to take back their freedom, to take back their lives.

A messenger approached.

"Western Cumorla has been secured, sir," he said.

"The Empire soldiers?" Akila asked.

"Fleeing to the east."

"How many civilian lives lost?"

"Three hundred, thus far."

Akila clenched his fists. It was less than expected, but each life lost was a weight on his conscience, another son or daughter dead, a mother, brother, sister, father butchered while defending this land's freedom.

He dismissed the messenger and signaled to his lieutenant to alert the final wave of militias. They would trap the invaders on the western entrance and treat them with the same courtesy with which they had treated his people. Not much would be left of them after that, and that brought great joy to Akila's heart.

Akila kicked his horse forward, leading the lieutenant and his men into battle. He rode down the hill and in through the northern

74

city gates, past balconied passageways, closed inns, and padlocked work shacks. He passed families huddled in corners, children lying facedown on the stone streets, and horses on the run without riders. The militias followed Akila without the city walls, hiding behind trenches to await the thousands of Empire soldiers that would soon flee through the gates and try to escape toward the harbor.

Not a one must escape, Akila had told his men this morning as he had ordered hundreds of men to stand guard at the docks. For even one escapee meant word would get back to Delos—and then the king would send tens of thousands of Empire soldiers to Haylon.

Minutes passed, and minutes more, until they had been lying in wait for nearly an hour, as twilight descended.

Then, suddenly, the first Empire soldier rode out on a horse, holding the Empire ensign, Akila saw.

"Long live King Claudius!" the soldier yelled.

Three flaming arrows hit him in the chest.

He fell off his horse, into the canal below the bridge.

Three more Empire soldiers followed, all felled, too, as they rode through the gates.

Soldier after soldier then trickled out of the city gates, and a brutal battle ensued.

Akila led the way with a fierce battle cry as night fell. All around him men were losing their lives to the cause of freedom, a freedom they would never see, but that perhaps their children would.

Akila gathered his most ruthless warriors to ride with him into the city, and he looked side to side to see them now, their horses thundering in his ears. He led the group of three hundred through the southern entrance, and then as they rode split them into four groups of fifty, each to search for Empire soldiers in different directions.

With torches and swords, Akila led his men down winding streets, stopping at every house, searching—hunting high and low, not a single enemy to be found. Almost at the end of their search, they happened upon a stable behind the high priest's mansion, and Akila thought it looked like an excellent hiding place for Empire soldiers.

As he was about to command his men to search the stable, the high priest stepped out from his house.

"Have you seen any Empire soldiers this way?" Akila asked, descending his horse.

"No," the priest said, his hands clasped as if in reverence in front of his body.

But there was something unsettling in the priest's eyes that made Akila think he was lying.

"Search the stable," Akila told his soldiers, and they immediately headed toward and entered the building.

There was a sudden uproar, and when Akila turned toward the commotion, the priest took off running down the street. Akila ran after him, but when he arrived at the street, he saw the priest galloping on a horse in the direction of the southern entrance.

Akila whistled, and once his horse was by his side, he hopped onto it and rode after the escapee. Through the city gates the priest went, with Akila on his heels, but Akila couldn't quite catch up to him.

Riding eastward, Akila whipped his horse onward relentlessly, his eyes on the escapee. He passed palm trees and hopped fences, rode through grassy fields and sand dunes. Following the priest down a steep sloping hill, it was then he saw a makeshift dock, hidden below a dome of trees. None of his men had been ordered to watch this dock because no one knew it was there.

To his dread, he saw the priest push away in a small sailboat, the wind catching the red sail immediately.

Almost there, Akila wondered if his horse would make the leap from the landing pier and into the boat, the distance increasing by the second. The horse's muscles tensed beneath him, but Akila drove it forward.

The horse leapt from the dock and into the vessel, skidding as it landed on the slippery wooden deck, throwing Akila off in the fall.

Slightly dazed from the rough landing, Akila rose to his feet and drew his sword.

The priest charged immediately, his sword held high, and he lunged and stabbed with the ferocity of a man who knew his life was at stake.

Akila dashed forward and slashed his blade toward the traitor, slicing him in the face. The man growled, dropped his sword, and whipped out a dagger, flinging it at Akila. But Akila saw it coming and blocked the dagger with his blade.

The priest spun and hurled a basket at Akila, then a wooden crate. Akila hit them away. Next, the priest grabbed a net and tossed it so Akila's sword hand became wrapped in it, and then he pulled on the net, causing Akila to stumble forward.

Coming at him, the priest picked up his sword and aimed it at Akila's chest, but Akila wore heavy armor and the man's sword slid off the metal like butter, causing the priest to stumble forward.

Taking advantage, Akila shook the net from off his arm and stabbed the priest.

He collapsed to the deck, dead.

Akila pulled his blade out of the priest's limp body and cleaned it on the net before sliding it back in its sheath.

Not wasting a second, he looked to the city walls, and seeing the black sky was turning navy blue, he realized he needed to return to his men, and quick. He sailed the boat back to the dock, set the boat on fire, and rode with all he had toward the eastern entrance.

Just as he arrived, pink graced the sky. Victory was called, and a new banner was placed atop the outer walls of Cumorla.

As bells of freedom tolled through the capital, Akila rode through the city's streets with his militia, men, women, and children cheering them on.

He looked toward the north and thought of his family members in Delos, still in bondage, and he knew in his heart that freedom was coming for them, too.

For here, for the first time in history, he stood on the first free land in the Empire.

The revolution had begun.

CHAPTER THIRTEEN

Ceres felt a pang of fear as she realized someone was following her. She quickened her pace on the rocky white pathway, lit by the morning sun, winding her way amidst green lawns and endless rows of flowers, her mind still reeling from her encounter the night before with Thanos. She paused and looked over her shoulder, listening for the footsteps she knew she had just heard.

Yet there was no one in sight.

Ceres froze and listened. She didn't have time for annoying games. She needed to get to the palace training ground with the weapons in the barrow before practice started, or Thanos would be weaponless.

Who could it be?

Overheated, she glanced up into the sky as a drop of sweat rolled down her forehead. The sun was a hot glowing disk already, and just like the gardens, she was withering. The muscles in her arms and shoulders started to burn, but she couldn't afford to rest. She was late as it was.

Pushing the heavy handcart, she picked up her pace, and when the footsteps came again, and she spun and saw no one, her irritation increased.

Finally, as she neared the gazebo, the footsteps grew louder, and when she glanced over her shoulder again, this time she spotted Stephania, wearing a red silk dress, a golden wreath in her golden hair.

Of course. The snooping princess.

"Hello, weapon girl," Stephania said, a slight frown on her face.

Ceres bowed her head and turned back around, eager to get away. But before Ceres could escape, Stephania stepped in front of her, blocking the narrow path.

"How does a girl become something as lowly as a weapon-keeper, I wonder?" Stephania asked, her hand hitting her hips.

"Thanos hired me," Ceres replied. "Now if you would so kindly—"

"You will address me as your highness!" Stephania snapped.

Ceres startled and she wanted to give the spoiled girl a piece of her mind, but instead, she kept her head down, reminding herself she wasn't here to protect her honor, only to fight for the revolution.

"Yes, your highness," she said.

"It is important you know your place, would you not agree?" Stephania said.

She walked a slow circle around Ceres, eyes probing, hands clasped behind her back, and fancy shoes clicking against the bricks as she strode.

"Since the day you arrived, I have been watching you. I will *always* be watching you. Do you hear?" Stephania said.

Ceres pinched her lips together so she wouldn't be tempted to say something disrespectful in return, although it was becoming increasingly difficult to remain silent.

"I see the way you look at Prince Thanos, but you would be foolish to think he would consider you anything but—"

"I can assure you—" Ceres started.

Stephania stepped so close to Ceres's face that their noses were an inch away, and then she whispered through gritted teeth, "Don't interrupt your superior when she is speaking!"

Ceres squeezed fingers around the cart's handles, her forearms now burning.

"Prince Thanos may have hired you, but as his future wife, it is my responsibility to ensure his associations are trustworthy," Stephania said.

Now Ceres couldn't hold back anymore.

"Thanos told me he wasn't going to marry you," she said.

Stephania flinched.

"Thanos is a smart man, but he is no good judge of character. He probably failed to learn what transgressions there might be in your past before he hired you."

Did Stephania know about how she killed the slaver and his guards? Ceres wondered, now considering she could lose her position at the palace and be punished for it if it came out.

"There are no transgressions in my past," Ceres said sternly.

Stephania laughed.

"Oh, come now. Everyone has done something in the past they are ashamed of," she said.

Stephania picked up a sword from the handcart and poked Ceres's leg with it. Oh, how Ceres wanted to give the rotten princess a lesson in swordsmanship, revealing how inept her clean, dainty, little monarch hands were. But she remained immovable.

"And believe me," Stephania said as she raised the blade to Ceres's face, a hair away. "If there is so much as a sliver of a transgression in your past, I will find out, and then I will have you thrown out of the palace, headfirst."

Stephania tossed the sword onto the ground next to Ceres's feet, the blade clattering as it landed.

"Thanos is mine, do you hear?" Stephania said. "He has been promised to me by the king and queen and if you get in the way of our marriage, I will personally slit your throat while you are sleeping in my future summer home."

Stephania shoved Ceres with her shoulder as she walked by, heading toward the palace training grounds.

*

The second Ceres arrived at the practice arena, she could sense that something was wrong. It wasn't that Stephania was glowering at her from beneath the willow trees, although their conversation was still swimming through Ceres's mind, irritating her to no end. It wasn't that it seemed the day would turn into the hottest one of the year, or that Thanos wasn't here yet, practicing.

As she rolled the handcart toward their weapon table, her eyes followed Lucious in the middle of the practice arena. He was clutching a bottle of wine in one hand, a sword in the other, and his new weapon-keeper knelt before him with a worried expression, while balancing an apple on his head. The weapon-keeper had several small cuts on his face, and one on his neck, Ceres saw.

"Stay...very...still," Lucious said, closing his eyes while pointing the tip of his sword toward the weapon-keeper's head.

The other royal warriors and their weapon-keepers stood watching, rolling their eyes, arms folded across chests.

Stepping closer, Ceres could see that Lucious's face and arms were bruised, one eye swollen and red. She couldn't remember him becoming injured yesterday at the Killings. Had something happened after the event?

She walked over to the table and started laying weapons out in preparation for when Thanos would arrive. Swords, daggers, a trident, a flogger.

From the corner of her eye, she saw Lucious stagger, causing the other royal warriors and a few weapon-keepers to laugh.

Lucious touched the tip of his sword to the weapon-keeper's nose, and the weapon-keeper winced with closed eyes as a drop of blood made its way into his mouth.

"Don't move a muscle or you could lose your head," Lucious said. "And you would have no one to blame but yourself."

This was insane, Ceres thought. Couldn't someone do something? She glanced at the others, but no one said a word or seemed to have any intent on helping Lucious's victim.

Next, Lucious raised his sword, but before he swung, the weapon-keeper whimpered and the apple fell from his head and onto the ground, bouncing on impact, rolling a few feet away.

"I told you to remain still!" Lucious snapped.

"I...I'm sorry," the weapon-keeper said, cowering backward, fright in his eyes.

"Get out of my sight, you useless piece of dung!" Lucious yelled.

The young man rose from his knees and scurried over to Lucious's weapon table. Just then, Thanos arrived.

"Good morrow," he said to Ceres, not having witnessed what just happened. "I trust you slept well?"

"Yes, thank you," Ceres said, now all of a sudden feeling much lighter from his presence.

She continued to place weapons on the table, but when he remained quiet, she looked over at him. To her surprise, she found that he was studying her face with eyes that seemed to want possess her, and when she raised an eyebrow at him, his lips tilted upward into a hint of a smile.

She felt her cheeks warm.

Without a word between them, he began helping her organize the weapons.

That's odd that he would help me, Ceres thought. He's a prince. Perhaps he was trying to show appreciation in return for how she had helped him at the Killings? He didn't have to do that, Ceres knew, though she did know one thing. When he showed kindness like this, it was becoming more and more difficult to reconcile the caring man before her with the arrogant man she had always thought he was.

Ceres glanced over to Stephania, and the princess's eyes were spewing hatred toward her. Surely, it couldn't be that Stephania was jealous of her? Thanos wouldn't take interest in a commoner, would he?

Ceres shook her head and laughed a bit, throwing the ridiculous thought out of her mind.

"What is it?" Thanos asked, smiling.

"Nothing," Ceres said. "So, what happened to Lucious anyway?"

"You mean the bruises?"

"Yes."

"The king had him beaten for how spinelessly he acted yesterday," Thanos said.

81

Even though she, too, thought Lucious a spineless imbecile, Ceres couldn't help but feel sorry for him. She had herself been bruised and battered countless times, and it wasn't something she wished upon anyone.

All of a sudden, Lucious yelled at his weapon-keeper, and just as she glanced up, she saw Lucious punching the young man in the stomach.

"Why isn't anyone doing anything?" Ceres asked.

Immediately, Thanos strode over to Lucious, stopping a few feet away.

"What are you trying to prove?" Thanos asked.

Lucious scoffed.

"Nothing."

Thanos took a threatening step toward Lucious.

"Why would I have anything to prove to anyone? I mean, look at you, anything is better than having a ratty, thin girl as a weapon-keeper," Lucious said with a scornful laugh.

"I suggest you treat your weapon-keeper with respect, and if you don't, I'm sure the king would see nothing wrong in leaving you to fend for yourself out in the arena," Thanos said.

"Is that a threat?" Lucious asked, eyes seething.

Just then a messenger arrived and handed Thanos a scroll. Thanos read it, and looking back toward Ceres, he gave her a nod before heading toward the palace.

Had he been summoned? Ceres wondered, not too thrilled about being left without any instruction.

An Empire soldier stepped into the center of the arena and listed in which order the royals would spar, with Lucious against Argus first.

"Finally!" Lucious said.

He flung the bottle of wine onto the ground, shattering it, and his weapon-keeper offered him a sword. He snatched it, and then with contrived enthusiasm, Ceres thought, he strode onto the practice arena where Argus waited.

The Empire soldier signaled the start of the match, and the royals began to spar. Lucious's first attack ended with his sword smashing into the ground, some onlookers snickering, others rolling their eyes. Lucious used his energy unwisely, Ceres saw, his jabs and lunges careless, with far too much effort.

The contenders took their places again, blade against blade, but within seconds of starting over, only a few hits in, Argus had hit Lucious's sword out of his hands and pointed his tip against Lucious's chest.

As soon as the Empire soldier named Argus the winner, Argus lowered his sword and jogged off the practice arena.

"Come on, cousin. Give me one more chance!" Lucious yelled after him. "I wasn't even trying!"

When Lucious saw Argus wouldn't entertain him, he turned to his own weapon-keeper.

"Xavier, spar with me," Lucious said.

"S...sire?" Xavier said with a nervous stutter. "I would, my lord, but I have no skill."

Angered, Lucious darted over to his weapon table, picked up a dagger, and stabbed Xavier in the abdomen.

Ceres's hand hit her mouth, and she gasped with the others as the weapon-keeper cried and fell to the ground, arms wrapped around his waist.

"Get the runt out of my sight!" Lucious yelled.

Within a few seconds, Empire soldiers hoisted the moaning weapon-keeper onto a stretcher and carried him away.

"What I don't understand," Lucious said, making his way over to Georgio's table, "is how I always get stuck with incompetence. Georgio, friend, lend me your boy."

Georgio stepped between his weapon-keeper and Lucious.

"Lucious, you know I hold you in high regard. But this is insanity. Go home," Georgio said with a chuckle, resting a hand on Lucious's shoulder.

"Get your pretty-boy hands off me!" Lucious yelled, whacking Georgio's arm away.

Yelling obscenities, Lucious walked over to another weapon-keeper, demanding he spar with him, but his master refused, too.

"Will no one fight me?" Lucious yelled, turning in a slow circle as his eyes scanned the bystanders. "Are you nothing but pitiful chicken droppings?"

With animosity in cold eyes, he continued to scrutinize the spectators, but most turned their eyes away.

Then he saw Ceres.

A pit formed in her stomach as he stomped toward her, pointing.

"You!" he yelled. "You will fight me!"

Ceres felt she would win a match against him, yet she was reluctant to accept, fearing she might hurt him, or make him look like the incompetent warrior he was in front of his peers. And if she made him look incompetent, she suspected Lucious would make certain she lost her position at the palace.

"I mean no disrespect, but I cannot fight you," she said.

"You will!" Lucious said. "In fact, I command you to spar with me."

She glanced at the others, some of them shaking their heads, others looking away, Stephania grinned wickedly. Could she refuse him? And what would happen if she did? Would Lucious fire her? Reason told her he probably would.

"Then I must accept the command," she said, thinking it might be better to accept than refuse him.

Lucious's face lit up.

"But first, may I fetch my sword from the blacksmith's chalet?" Ceres asked, thinking of her father's sword.

"Hurry along, little rat," Lucious said.

His comment exasperated her, but she would not let insulting words from a drunken coward affect her.

Excited as a spring day to finally be able to use her sword in real one-on-one combat, Ceres ran to the blacksmith's chalet and located her sword in the loft where she had left it. She sprinted back to the practice arena and took her spot across Lucious, who was standing ready with his own sword.

Lucious took one look at Ceres's sword, and his jaw dropped open.

"Where would a rodent like you get a weapon like that?" he asked with covetous eyes.

"My father gave it to me."

"Well, what a fool he must have been," Lucious said.

"And why is that?" Ceres asked.

"Today I will triumph over you, and when I do, your weapon will be mine."

Lucious lunged at Ceres, their blades colliding. Although Lucious was rather lacking in muscularity, gangly even, he was strong. After blocking a few blows, she began to doubt whether or not she would be able to win.

He slashed again but she resisted, and sword pressing against sword, they encircled as they stared into each other's eyes. She could see his hatred for her in those hazel irises, and she wondered what she possibly could have done to deserve it.

He shoved her hard so she had to move back several steps so as not to fall, and then he hacked at her from above, as she blocked from below.

A low rumble of excitement made its way through the bystanders.

Lunging, she slashed, but he retreated and wobbled a bit, his brow misted with sweat, his shoulders tense.

But then Lucious's eyes darkened, and he swung at her, rashly. She jumped over his blade, and just as she landed, she kicked him in the abdomen so he fell onto his back.

He didn't move for a moment, and Ceres wondered if he was unconscious. But a sudden shriek spilled out of his lips and he sat up. Leaning on his sword, he climbed to his feet while mumbling something underneath his breath.

"You're better than I thought, I'll give you that," Lucious said. "But I was going easy on you. Now I'm finished playing games, and you, little rat, must die."

Sweat stung Ceres's eyes, and she raised her sword as she exhaled several forceful breaths. She could feel Stephania's glare at the back of her head, and it made her want to triumph all the more.

Coming at her, Lucious attacked with all his might. She pretended she would meet him head on, but then swerved last minute and kicked her legs between his, and he tumbled to the ground onto his belly.

His sword skidded across the ground, stopping a few feet away, and then there was utter silence.

Lucious rolled onto his back. Ceres stood above him, holding the tip of her sword at his throat, waiting for the Empire soldier to call the winner.

But the soldier remained silent.

She looked up, and the Empire soldier still said nothing, an impassive expression on his face.

Glowering, Lucious climbed to a standing position and spit on the ground next to Ceres's feet.

"I refuse to acknowledge a girl's victory," he said.

Ceres took a step forward.

"I won fair and square," she said.

Lucious raised his hand and backhanded her across the cheek, the demoralizing assault causing several observers to gasp. Without even a second thought, acting only on rage and impulse, Ceres slapped him in return.

Right as her hand hit his face, she knew it was a huge mistake; yet there was not a thing she could do to take it back. Everyone had seen it, and although she wasn't quite certain what the punishment was for striking a royal, she knew it would be severe.

Holding his cheek, Lucious looked at her with wide, surprised eyes and for a few moments, it was as if time had frozen.

"Arrest her!" he yelled, pointing at her.

Ceres faltered a few steps back, time passing as if in a nightmare. But her mind seemed to not want to function, and before she could even think what to do or what to say, two Empire soldiers had grabbed her arms.

A moment later they were dragging her away, far from here, and far from the life she had almost had.

CHAPTER FOURTEEN

"Rexus!"

Rexus turned to see a frantic Nesos sprinting toward him, and his heart flooded with dread. Nesos had been dispatched on an important mission, so his being here couldn't be good, Rexus knew.

Nesos skidded to a halt right in front of Rexus, dust stirring the air, and rested hands on knees while he panted.

"I just came... from northern Delos and... the Empire soldiers are everywhere... saying new laws are being enacted, they are hauling off... firstborn men, slaughtering... anyone who refuses," Nesos said, still breathless, sweat running down his face.

Rexus's blood curdled. He shot to his feet and took off at a run toward the main entrance of the castle. He had to warn the others.

"Next they will attack Delos east, then west...and finally south," Nesos said, trailing after him.

Rexus had an idea.

"Take with you a few men and send every dove we have to warn our supporters," he said. "Ask them to meet below North Square as soon as possible and with as many weapons as they can carry. We will free these firstborns so they can join the rebellion. I will gather the supporters here and ride out immediately."

"Right away," Nesos said.

It begins here, Rexus thought as he ran toward the others. Today they would make a stand and kill in the name of freedom.

Within moments Rexus had over a hundred men and fifty women assembled in front of the cascading waterfall, ready on horses, weapons in hand. As he explained the plan to the revolutionaries, he saw fear in their eyes. A fearful warrior would not win any battles, he knew. And so he stood before them to speak.

"I see in each of your eyes the terror of death," Rexus said.

"Fear you not death?" a man yelled from the crowd.

"Yes, I do. I have no wish to die. But more than fearing death, my deepest fear is living the rest of my life on my knees," Rexus said. "More than fearing death, I fear I will never know freedom. And these firstborn men can help us attain that."

"But we have children!" a woman yelled. "They will be punished for our rebellion!"

"I have no children of my own, but I know the fear of losing someone dear. If we win, your children and your children's children will never know oppression the way we have. And would you not rather your children follow in your example of courage than your example of fear?" he said.

The militia grew ghostly silent, and nothing but the roar of the waterfall and the occasional neighing of a horse could be heard.

"Do not fool yourselves into believing the Empire will give you liberty," Rexus said.

"I, like many here, are with you, friend," a man shouted. "But do you think we have a real chance at winning this war?"

"The war will not be won today," Rexus continued. "Not tomorrow, even. But eventually, we *will* win. A people who demands freedom will in the end claim it."

Heads nodded and a few lifted weapons into the air.

"We are few. They are many," another man said.

"We, the oppressed, outnumber the oppressors a hundred to one, and as soon as we have enough supporters, we will triumph!" Rexus said.

"They will never permit us to usurp the throne," a woman said.

"Permit?" Rexus said. "You do not need permission from any king, queen, or royal to free yourselves from the bonds of oppression. Today, and every day from now on, give yourselves permission and fight to take back your liberty!"

One by one, the rebels raised weapons into the air, soon the sound of their cheers overpowering the waterfall.

The time, Rexus knew, had come.

*

As he rode toward Delos, followed by his men, the sound of the horses galloping in his ears, Rexus's thoughts turned toward Ceres. She had looked so thin and vulnerable when he saw her last, and his heart had nearly burst with emotion. Like every time before, he had been such a fool—had only kissed her briefly when he wanted to take her into his arms and keep her there forever.

From atop his horse, he saw the palace in the distance, and it haunted him to think of her alone amidst a sea of corruption, amidst the very wolves they fought against, her life endangered at every turn. He wanted to ride like the wind and save Ceres from such a place.

Ever since he could remember, he had wanted to marry Ceres; indeed, a large part of his motivation to join the rebellion was so that their future children could live in freedom. Yet, every time he saw her, his tongue twisted into a thousand knots, and he had never been able to say those words to her. He was a fool.

Riding to an uncertain fate, he suddenly realized that it wasn't true what he had said to the rebels just minutes ago. His deepest fear wasn't living the rest of his life on his knees. His deepest fear was that Ceres would have to do that, and that they might never have the chance to be together.

*

Rexus arrived at the North Square with his troops, heavy fog a dense curtain around him, the city of Delos breathing like a ghost town. The trip had been more gruesome than he could ever have imagined—bodies lying facedown, contorted in unnatural position, mothers holding their dead children, sobbing, houses pillaged and plundered, blood flowing down the cobblestone streets.

And this, he knew, was just the beginning.

The scout he had sent out reported that there were over a thousand Empire soldiers in the piazza—though it was difficult to see clearly in such weather. At the moment, the soldiers were preparing to eat, so it would be the perfect time to attack.

Rexus glanced back at noble faces and dear friends. Not a one had proper armor like the Empire soldiers had, although most had been trained sufficiently in battle. There was no way this small army of roughly two hundred could triumph over a thousand Empire soldiers. Had he led these brave men and women into a suicide mission? he wondered.

If the doves had arrived to their destinations, a few more men and women would be on their way, he knew, perhaps adding another hundred to the militia, but that was still not nearly enough to defeat a thousand.

"But hundreds upon hundreds of young men—firstborns—are locked up in wagons in the center of the piazza," the scout told Rexus.

"Hundreds, you say?" Rexus asked, his heart growing hopeful.

The scout nodded.

Rexus named thirty men, himself included, whose main goal would be to break open the locks of the wagons and invite the firstborns to fight with them, increasing the rebellion's numbers. The other men and women would fight off the Empire soldiers, distracting them from noticing their new recruits were being stolen.

By the time Rexus had solidified the plan, more than a hundred additional revolutionaries had arrived, ready to fight with them.

Rexus ordered Nesos, the scout, and half the militia to attack from the north, and then he waited with nervous patience until the scout returned, saying the rebels had arrived safely at the other side of North Square.

This was a significant moment, he thought. For centuries, the oppression had been a curse over the land, a chain around hundreds of thousands of people's necks.

Trembling, yet resolute, Rexus raised his sword.

"For freedom!" he yelled as he led the revolutionaries into battle.

As they rode toward the square, horse hooves pounding against the rocks below, every rebel held breaths of dread, but also breaths of hope, Rexus could feel.

I must be strong for them, he thought, despite the weakness that pollutes my heart.

And so he willed his horse forward even though he feared death would take him if he didn't stop.

Rexus rode his horse as far as he could onto the battlefield, toward the wagons filled with firstborns, until the congestion of fighters prevented him from riding any further. He let out a great battle cry as he threw himself into the fray.

Rexus raised his sword and stabbed one soldier through the heart, sliced another's throat, and drove his sword through a third's abdomen, the cries of wounded men all around him.

An Empire soldier pulled Rexus from his horse and came at him with his sword, but Rexus ducked and then kicked the soldier in the knee, a sickening crack of bone.

The next Empire soldier—a monster of a man—hit Rexus's sword out of his hand. Weaponless, Rexus flung himself at the soldier, digging thumbs into the man's eyes.

The giant shrieked and socked Rexus in the stomach so he fell to the ground. Another soldier came at Rexus, and yet another.

Soon he was surrounded, three against one.

He saw his sword only a few feet away and scurried on hands and knees for it, but a soldier stood in his way. Rexus snatched the dagger from his boot and flung it into the soldier's neck before grabbing his sword and hopping to his feet.

The giant, now with a spear in his hands, sprang toward Rexus. Rexus hopped back and hacked the spear to the ground and then stepped on it, breaking it. With all his force, he kicked the brute in the abdomen. Nothing happened. Instead, Rexus stabbed his opponent in the foot, but he was punished with a fist to the side of his head, and he went crashing to the ground, his ear throbbing.

He staggered to his feet, his surroundings spinning, and suddenly, he felt a sharp pain in his arm, warm blood spilling out from the fresh wound. He cried out.

After a moment he was able to see clearly, and he plunged his sword into the giant's lower abdomen. The Empire soldier fell to his knees and Rexus stepped aside as the soldier fell forward onto his face.

Shouts caught his attention, and he looked up to see the wagons crammed with the firstborn men a mere twenty feet away. He ran over to them, slashing more Empire soldiers on the way, and slashed the lock off the first door.

"Fight with us!" he yelled as the young men streamed out. "Win your freedom!"

Rexus ran to the next wagon, and the next, smashing the locks open, releasing as many firstborns as were imprisoned, asking them to fight. Most picked up swords of fallen soldiers and joined in the battle.

As the fog lightened, Rexus was saddened to see several of his men lay fallen on the cobblestones, his allies in eternity, his friends no more. But to his great joy, many more of the Empire soldiers lay lifeless, too.

"Retreat!" Rexus cried, seeing that he had accomplished his mission.

A horn blared through the fog, echoing in the streets, and his people fled from the battle, scattering into side alleyways, vanishing down main roads, raising hands into the air, their victory cries echoing through the streets.

He looked into the faces of the living—now friends for life—and he could see a fire kindled within each of their eyes. It was the spirit of the revolution. And soon that flicker would turn into a fiery inferno that would destroy the entire Empire.

Everything was about to change.

CHAPTER FIFTEEN

Ceres sat on the cold stone dungeon floor and watched the small boy beside her, squirming in pain, and wondered if he would live. He lay there, belly down, his pale skin white in the dimness, eyes halfway open, still recovering from a flogging in the market. He was awaiting his sentence, just like everyone else in this dungeon.

Just like her.

She looked around to see the cell filled with men, women, and children, some chained to the wall, others free to roam around. It was dark in here, and the smell of urine was even more prominent here than in the slaver cart, with no breeze to carry away the stench. The stone walls were slick with grime and dried blood, the ceiling looming over them like the weight of the world, barely high enough for her to stand fully erect in, and the floor was covered in smeared feces and mouse-droppings.

Worriedly, Ceres glanced down at the boy again. He hadn't moved from his position since she had been thrown in here yesterday, but his chest was still rising and sinking with silent breaths.

With the sun beaming in through the small barred window, she saw that the wounds on his back were healing with the fabric of his tunic stuck to it. Ceres wanted to do something—anything—to relieve his pain, but she had already asked to help him several times and there had been no response, not even a flicker in his pale blue eyes.

Ceres stood and tucked herself into the corner, eyes swollen from crying, mouth and throat parched from thirst. She shouldn't have hit a royal across the face, she knew that, but when she had done it, she had only reacted.

Would Thanos come for her? she wondered. Or were his promises just as rotten as all the other royals'?

The pregnant woman sitting opposite her rubbed her swollen belly, moaning softly, and Ceres wondered if she had gone into labor. Perhaps the woman would have to give birth in this wretched hole. She looked down at the little boy again and her heart ached when she considered it wasn't many years since Sartes was that size, and remembered how she used to sing lullabies to him until he fell asleep.

She tensed up when she noticed the silhouettes of two prisoners approaching before her.

"Who is that boy to you?" a gruff voice asked.

Ceres looked up. One of the men had a dirty, bearded face with angry blue eyes, the other was a bald man, muscular as a combatlord, the skin below his eyes covered in swirling black tattoos. The robust one smashed his knuckles together and they cracked, and the chain around his ankle clattered as he moved.

"No one," she said, looking away.

The bearded man leaned hands against the wall behind her on either side, confining her, his raunchy breath wafting into her face.

"You're lying," he said. "I saw the way you looked at him."

"I'm not lying," Ceres said. "But if I were, it wouldn't make one bit of difference to you or anyone else in here. We'd still be stuck in this prison, awaiting our punishments."

"When we ask you a question, we expect an honest answer," the tattooed man said, stepping forward, his chain rattling again. "Or are you too good for us?"

Ceres knew that playing nice or trying to avoid the bullies wasn't going to make them leave her alone.

As quickly as she could, she ducked, and darted past the thugs so she could go to the other side of the room where their chains wouldn't reach. But she didn't get far.

The tattooed man lifted his leg and the chain with it, catching Ceres's legs, causing her to trip and fall on her face. The bearded man stepped on the boy's back, and the little one shrieked in pain.

Ceres tried to rise to her feet, but the tattooed man wound his chain around her neck and pulled.

"Let the boy...go," she croaked, barely able to speak.

The boy's cries pierced straight to her heart, and she tugged on the chain, trying to free herself.

The tattooed man tugged even harder, until she couldn't breathe.

"You do care, don't you? Now, because you lied, the boy will bleed to death," the bearded man hissed.

He gave the boy a swift kick in the back, the child's cry filling the crammed cell, the other prisoners turning their heads away, some weeping quietly.

Ceres felt her body come alive, a surge of power overcoming her like a storm. Without even knowing what she was doing, she found herself strengthening her grip around the chain and snapping it in two.

The bearded man stared back at her, stunned, as if he had seen a ghost rise from the dead.

Free from the chain, Ceres stood, took hold of the chain, and whipped the bearded man, again and again, until he cowered in the corner, begging for mercy.

With her insides alight, she spun around and faced the tattooed man, the force within still feeding her body the strength she needed to stop the aggressors.

"If you touch him, or me, or any of the people in here one more time, I will kill you with my bare hands, you hear?" she said, pointing at him.

But this one growled and threw himself at her. She raised her palms, feeling the heat burning within, and without her touching him he went flying into the wall across the room with a thud and collapsed onto the ground, unconscious.

A tense silence fell, as Ceres felt all the eyes in the room on her.

"What force is that?" the pregnant woman asked.

Ceres glanced over at her, then looked at the others; everyone in the cell was dumbfounded.

The little boy sat up and winced, and Ceres kneeled by his side.

"You need rest," she said.

Now that the fabric had torn from the boy's back, she could also see puss between the blood. If his wounds weren't cleaned, he would die of the infection, she knew.

"How did you do that?" the boy asked.

Everyone's eyes were still on Ceres, wanting to know the answer to that question.

It was an answer she wanted to know herself.

"I...don't know," she said. "It just...overcame me when I saw what he was doing to you."

The boy paused and as he lay back down, with weary eyes, he said, "Thank you."

"Ceres," came a sudden whisper in the darkness. "Ceres!"

Ceres turned and looked through the bars of the cell and saw the form of a person wearing a hooded cape, the torches in the hallway illuminating the black material. Was it a servant boy sent by Thanos? she wondered.

Careful not to step on fingers and toes, Ceres made her way over to the stranger. He removed the hood, and to her astonishment and joy, she saw that it was Sartes.

"How did you find me? What are you doing here?" she asked, her hands gripping the bars, her chest brimming with joy—and trepidation.

"The blacksmith told me you were here, and I had to see you," he whispered, tears in his eyes. "I've been so worried for you."

She reached a hand through the bars and pressed a palm to his cheek.

"Sweet Sartes, I am doing well."

"This is not well," he said, his face etched with graveness.

"It is well enough. At least they haven't said anything about…"

She stopped herself from speaking the unspeakable, not wanting to worry Sartes.

"If they kill you, Ceres, I will…I will…"

"Shush, now. They will do no such thing." She lowered her voice several notches before whispering, "How is the rebellion?"

"There was a battle in northern Delos yesterday, a huge one. We won."

She smiled.

"So it has begun," she said.

"Nesos is fighting as we speak. He was injured yesterday, but not enough to keep him in bed."

Ceres smiled a little.

"Always the tough one. And Rexus?" she asked.

"He is well, too. He misses you."

Hearing Sartes say that nearly brought Ceres to tears. Oh, how she missed Rexus, too.

Sartes leaned closer, his cape covering his arm, and then she peered down when she felt a sharp, cold object against her hand—a dagger. Without a word, only the silent understanding between them, she took the dagger and stuffed it down the front of her pants and then covered it with her shirt.

"I have to go before someone sees me," Sartes said.

She nodded, and reached tender arms through the bars.

"I love you, Sartes. Remember that."

"I love you, too. Be well."

Just as he vanished down the hallway, passing him, she saw the warden approach. She huddled back in the corner next to the boy, her hand stroking his hair, and the warden unlocked the door and stepped into the prison.

"Listen up, criminals. Here are the names of those who will be executed on the day after the morrow at sunrise: Apollo."

The boy let out a gasp, and Ceres felt him start to tremble beneath her hands.

"…Trinity…" the warden continued.

The pregnant woman cringed and swooped her arms around her swollen belly.

"…Ceres…"

Ceres felt a sudden sense of panic overtake her.

"…and Ichabod."

A man chained to the far end of the cell buried his face in his hands and sobbed quietly.

95

The warden turned on his feet and exited the cell, locking it behind him, nothing but the sound of his heavy footsteps marching away.

And with those few words, her death loomed.

CHAPTER SIXTEEN

Thanos stormed into the throne room, clutching the scroll signed by the king—the abominable document which contained Ceres's execution orders. His heart was thundering against his ribs as his feet pounded the white marble floor beneath them, rage churning through him from head to toe.

Thanos had always thought this room was spacious beyond reason, the arched ceilings ridiculously high, the distance from the massive bronze door to the two thrones at the end nothing but wasted space. Or tainted space. The throne room was the place where all rules were forged, and to Thanos, this was where all the inequality originated.

Advisors and dignitaries sat between red marble pillars on intricately carved wooden seats on either side of the room, twirling their golden rings, wearing their fine apparel, proudly displaying colored sashes, which ranked them according to their importance.

The sun shone in through stained-glass windows, blinding him every few steps, but that didn't prevent him from glaring at the king who sat on his golden seat at the end of the room. Soon, Thanos stood at the bottom of the staircase below the thrones. He hurled the execution order at the feet of the king and queen, who were at the moment speaking with the minister of trade.

"I demand you recant this execution order at once!" Thanos said.

The king looked up with exhausted eyes.

"You shall wait your turn, nephew."

"There is no time. Ceres is to be executed on the morrow!" Thanos said.

The king huffed and shooed the minister away. Once the minister had left, the king looked at Thanos.

"Ceres, *my* weapon-keeper, might I remind you, was thrown in prison by Lucious, and now she is being sentenced to death?" Thanos said.

"Yes, she smote a royal, and that is, by law, punishable by public execution," the king said.

"Did you know Lucious backhanded her first? And all because she triumphed in a sword fight he demanded?"

"How does this commoner know how to wield a sword?" the queen asked. "It is against the laws of the land to do so."

The king nodded, and the advisors mumbled in agreement.

"Her father worked as a swordsmith here at the palace," Thanos said.

"If he taught her how to wield the sword, they should both be executed on the spot," the queen said.

"How can you be a good swordsmith unless you know how to wield a sword?" Thanos pressed. "Being a swordsmith is not forbidden for a woman."

"This is not about being a swordsmith, or a swordsman, Thanos. This is about a commoner assaulting a royal on royal grounds," the king said.

The queen laid a hand over the king's.

"If I didn't know Thanos was promised to Stephania, I would think he was taking an interest in this girl," she said.

"I take no interest in her other than that she is the best weapon-keeper I have had," Thanos lied.

"Stephania said she had seen you on the palace training ground with…what was the servant girl's name?" the queen asked.

"Ceres," Thanos said.

"Yes, Ceres. And Stephania said you held her arm."

"The girl doesn't have a home, and so I offered her to stay in the southern summer cottage for the time being," Thanos said.

"And who gave you that authority?" the queen asked.

"You know as well as I do that it used to be my parents' cottage, and it hasn't been used since they passed away," Thanos said.

"Stephania is a bright young lady with dignity and integrity, and she says she doesn't trust this strange girl. Has Ceres any credentials? Any official papers? She could be an assassin working for the rebellion for all we know," the queen said, working herself into a tizzy.

"Now, dear, let's not get all carried away. Do you really think the rebellion would send a female assassin?" the king said.

"Perhaps not," the queen replied. "Or perhaps they would, thinking a gullible young prince like Thanos would fall for a feisty warrior woman who sides with him against his family."

"No matter. The girl has her sentence, and to protect Lucious's honor, it will be carried through," the king said.

"You didn't think of protecting him when you sent him to compete in the Killings!" Thanos said.

The king scooted forward to the edge of his seat and pointed at Thanos, his eyes darkened with ire.

"Boy, you live in our palace and at the mercy and generosity of the queen and me. Do you really mean to defy us yet again?" he asked.

Thanos pointed to the Empire's banner to the right of the king.

"Freedom and justice to every citizen!" he bellowed, his voice echoing through the room. "The responsibility of the country's leaders is to protect the freedom of the people and to rule in justice. This is not justice."

"Stop with this nonsense," the king said. "The decision is final, and no amount of begging or senseless reasoning from you will change that."

"Then you must also imprison and sentence Lucious to death for what he did," Thanos said.

"Although I would not mourn the loss of Lucious for one solitary second, I will follow the laws of this land," the king said. "And if you interfere with my decision in any way, you will be expelled from court. Now leave so I can use my time on matters of importance."

Fuming, Thanos turned on his heels and tore out of the throne room, his pulse in his ears.

After he had marched back outside to the practice arena, he picked up a longsword. He went at a dummy long and hard, until there was nothing left but the wooden beam holding it, and then he hacked away at that, too.

Standing with the sword in his hands, he stood frozen as he panted for a long while, and then he flung the weapon as far as he could into the palace gardens.

How could the king possibly say he was serving justice? he wondered. Justice would mean every person had the same rights, privileges, and punishments, and Thanos knew that wasn't the case in the least.

He walked to the gazebo and slumped on a bench, his temple resting against his hands.

Ceres—what was it with her? Why did he need her the way he needed air? She had come into his life a breath of fresh air, her green eyes sparkling with wonder, her pale pink lips speaking words he knew he would never tire of, a quiet strength in her lithe body laced with vulnerability. She wasn't like the girls at court who would babble on about mindless subjects and gossip about others only to make themselves look better. Ceres had a depth to her, and every part of her was genuine, not a speck of pretentiousness to be found. And it was as if she saw what he needed even before he knew it himself—a sixth sense perhaps?

He stood up and paced back and forth in the gazebo for several minutes, wondering what to do.

When they had stood below the Stade, awaiting the Killings, he had asked her if he could trust her with his life. She had said yes. And although her voice had faltered with the answer, he knew she would sacrifice herself to save him if it ever came to that.

If he saved her, he would be kicked out of the palace. If he left her to her fate, he wouldn't be able to live with himself.

He pulled his shoulders back and took a deep breath.

He knew what he needed to do.

CHAPTER SEVENTEEN

Although her eyes and limbs were heavy, Ceres, despite her exhaustion, hadn't slept a wink all night. The heavens were slowly lightening, she could see from the small barred window, and how she wished they wouldn't. With morning came her last few moments, and in less than an hour, she knew, she would be dead.

"Are you afraid?" Apollo asked, his head resting in her lap as she stroked his blond hair.

She looked at him and thought of lying. But she couldn't.

"Yes. Are you?" Ceres said.

He nodded, a tear in his eye.

She could feel him quivering beneath her touch, or was it her hand that was trembling so?

The pregnant woman looked at Ceres with alarm in her eyes when the faint sound of footsteps came from the hallway. The distant noise came closer and closer until Ceres could hear nothing but the drum of marching men, and before she knew it, the warden stood before the cell, unlocking it.

"Apollo, Trinity, Ceres, and Ichabod, come with me," he said, several other Empire soldiers waiting behind him.

With hands that barely would move like she commanded them to, Ceres helped Apollo stand up. Fully erect, the boy reached only to just above her waist, Ceres noticed, and she thought it an awful shame that he would never get to grow up to be the man he might have become.

When she let go of him, his legs gave out from under him and he collapsed to the floor.

"Sorry," Apollo said with doleful eyes.

Crouching beside the boy, tears burning at the back of her eyes, Ceres shot the warden an ugly glare and helped Apollo to his feet again. Careful not to touch the wounds on his back, she supported him as they went into the dim, torch-lit hallway, the other two prisoners following behind them.

The warden jerked Apollo to the front, a soldier on each side holding the boy's arms so he wouldn't collapse. Ceres, trying to calm her shuddering legs, was next, and behind her, Trinity, and the old man Ichabod. The chains rattled when the Empire soldiers shackled Ceres's and the others' ankles and wrists, and once the prisoners had been chained, two Empire soldiers guarded each of them, one on either side. Trinity rocked back and forth, holding her belly, and then Ceres heard that she started to sing an old lullaby—the exact one Ceres used to sing to Sartes to make him fall asleep.

Ceres could no longer hold back the tears, and at the thought of her brothers, of Rexus, it was as if her heart broke in two. Never would she see them again, never would she joke with them, break bread with them, spar with them. Those had been such happy times, she remembered, even though they had been tainted by her mother's cruelty. But she loved them, and she wondered if they truly knew that.

Down the hallway Ceres walked, her feet feeling like blocks of stone as chains dragged on the floor, the beautiful tune of the pregnant woman guiding her steps. Climbing the stairs out of the dungeon, Ceres saw that it was slightly dark out, a few stars still twinkling above, refusing to give up their light in the pre-dawn heavens. An open horse-pulled wagon stood in the courtyard, and Ceres was shoved into the cart with the other prisoners, the Empire soldiers' whips causing her to cower, causing her to hate the Empire even more.

When Apollo was unable to climb into the wagon by himself, an Empire soldier picked the boy up and flung him into the cart so he hit his head against the side of the wagon, a yelp escaping his lips as his head was thrust backwards with a cracking sound.

"How could you be so cruel?" Ceres yelled at the Empire soldier, before turning her attention to Apollo.

She scooted closer to the boy, staring helplessly at the unnatural bend in his neck, and ever so carefully, she lifted his bleeding head into her lap.

"Apollo?" she croaked, dread filling her chest when she felt how lifeless his body had suddenly become.

"I can't see..." Apollo whispered with a hoarse voice, his eyes glazed with tears. "I...can't...I can't feel my legs."

She leaned forward and kissed his forehead, and seeing he was struggling to breathe, she wanted to help him. But all she could do was to take his small, cold hand in hers.

"I'm here," Ceres said, the words almost getting caught in her throat, tears dripping down onto his filthy, torn tunic.

"Promise to hold my hand...until I am...dead," Apollo stammered.

Ceres, unable to speak a word, just nodded and squeezed his hand in her own, gently stroking the blond hairs off his sweaty forehead.

His eyes fluttered before they shut, and then she noticed that his chest stopped rising and falling as his face yielded to the mask of death.

She sobbed once and brought his hand to her lips before placing it carefully on his chest. Now, at least, he wouldn't have to face decapitation, she thought. He was free.

As they rode through the crowd, she couldn't stop looking at the poor boy, his small lips, his eyelashes, the freckles on his nose. She wanted him to know she was still thinking of him and that she wouldn't leave him alone in the cart, at the mercy of the Empire soldiers that stole his freedom and his life. Perhaps she needed him in some small way, too, to remind her that there weren't only cruel people in this world, and that innocence and kindness were still more beautiful than any power on earth.

The wagon bumped past a blur of hateful words and angry faces, but she kept her eyes on Apollo's peaceful expression. Not even when a rotten tomato hit Ceres in the cheek did she tear her gaze from him.

The cart slowed to a stop in front of the wooden scaffold, and the prisoners were commanded to leave the wagon. However, Ceres refused to leave Apollo, clinging to him.

An Empire soldier, the one who had thrown him, grabbed Apollo by his legs and jerked him out of the wagon from Ceres's arms.

"Murderer!" she cried at the top of her lungs, tears spilling out of her eyes.

The soldier tossed Apollo onto a stack of hay, and then started toward Ceres, but she scuttled into the wagon's corner, refusing to get out.

Following after her, the Empire soldier that had just had his appalling hands on Apollo stepped into the wagon. She would not allow him to get away with murdering such an innocent boy. Seeing the other Empire soldiers were busy forcing the other prisoners up the stairs to the scaffold, she saw a chance to avenge him. She might die trying—but she was about to die anyway.

When the soldier leaned forward to haul her out of the cart, Ceres looped the shackles bound to her wrists around his neck and pulled with all her might.

On his back, the soldier croaked and kicked arms and legs, his filthy fingers tugging at the chain, his face turning red.

But Ceres refused to let the killer go, pulling harder until his face turned purple.

In what seemed like a last-ditch effort to save his life, the soldier's hands strained toward Ceres's neck. She blocked with her elbows, and just as she heard other Empire soldiers clamoring, scurrying toward the wagon, the man in her arms went limp.

Even after she knew he was dead, she kept the chain taut for as long as she could, until two Empire soldiers tore her out of the wagon and forced her to the bottom of the stairwell leading up to the scaffold.

One of the soldiers pulled out a dagger and pressed the tip to her back, the blade piercing her skin a little. She took a step. And then one more.

Her feet in a disoriented march, Ceres climbed the stairs after the others, the clamors of the crowd a distant tempest, and just as she arrived at the top, she was released from her chains.

Her heart hammered against her ribs, she vaguely noticed, and her throat was dry, her eyes wet. Had the crowd grown silent? she wondered, unable to tell above the roar of her trepidation.

An Empire soldier pulled her hands behind her back, tying them. She didn't resist. There was nothing more to resist now, she knew. She might as well let death take her.

The soldier shoved her in the direction of a man wearing a white hooded cloak, holding an axe—her executioner.

She was ordered to kneel before a wooden block, but when she didn't respond right away, the soldier pushed her to her knees, her head falling forward. With blurred vision, she looked up and out into the crowd, her entire body trembling, her stomach churning with nausea.

"Do you have any last words?" the executioner asked.

She remained frozen, trying to grasp this really was it. Her life, was it over? No. It couldn't be. It had gone so fast, too fast, and suddenly, there was no more time.

"Well, have you something to say, girl?" the executioner pressed.

She did have something to say, but the words would not formulate in her mind.

The crowd grew silent, all eyes on her, and then the executioner blindfolded her.

On her knees, she reached forward, feeling for the block, sensing its smoothness beneath her fingertips, and resigned to her death, she leaned forward and rested her chin on the wooden edge.

Father, she thought. Sartes. Nesos.

Rexus.

Then, to her disbelief, an image of Thanos formed in her mind, and she finally realized that even though she loved Rexus, she had fallen for Thanos, too.

And just as she grasped that, she hated herself for it. She was happy he would never find out.

She swallowed the tears back, exhaled a breath, and the crowd went silent as she waited for it all to be over.

CHAPTER EIGHTEEN

Rexus was filled with rage as he lay on a rooftop and watched thousands of citizens being held captive in Blackrock Square, surrounded by Empire soldiers who encircled the outer edge of the piazza, preventing escape. Standing before them atop a platform, General Draco was reading the king's proclamation, and each word deepened the rage in Rexus's heart. They were preparing to take away more firstborns, the best men the people had to offer. He tightened his grip on his sword, preparing for battle.

Yet seeing so many Empire soldiers, Rexus began to second-guess his decision to lead the revolutionaries into yet another battle they weren't entirely prepared for. The rebellion had grown, yes, but it was still barely over a thousand men. The only way to victory today was if the citizens below joined in and helped attack the enemy.

But would they?

When General Draco finished reading, he looked up and his narrow eyes raked the crowd.

"Before we collect the firstborns—a warning. Rebellion does not come without punishment!" he yelled.

He nodded toward his lieutenant, and the lieutenant opened one of the slaver carts that stood behind the platform. Rexus squinted his eyes, wondering who could be inside.

He was stunned to see captured revolutionaries hauled out of the wagon, Empire soldiers beating them with clubs toward the podium. Rexus felt as if he were stabbed in the heart. One of the twelve groups he had dispatched had been captured.

The soldiers chained the prisoners atop the platform and gagged them, and Rexus's ire deepened as he watched them dragging a kicking and screaming Anka up to the podium, chaining her to a pole, too, her clothes bloody, her face bruised.

Rexus narrowed his eyes, the sight of Anka up there—Ceres's friend—causing his blood to boil with fury.

"Lead us to the hiding place of the rebellion, and I will let these people live!" General Draco shouted to the crowd, his voice booming through the square. "Say nothing, and after these traitors have been tortured and killed, I will seize twenty of you, and then twenty more, and yet another twenty, until someone speaks!"

Clamors of panic went through the crowd as frightened mothers embraced their children. Yet the piazza remained silent, no one willing to offer up information.

General Draco nodded, and twenty Empire soldiers marched up onto the platform, holding lit torches, taking their places beside the prisoners. When the general nodded again, the soldiers pressed the torches to the revolutionaries' faces. Each man and woman screamed, the shrieks of pain burning Rexus's ears.

The onlookers raged in disapproval, but the Empire soldiers standing amidst the crowd forced protesters into silence with clubs, spears, and whips.

Incensed, Rexus knew he could wait no longer. Ready or not, the time had come.

Rexus jumped down from the roof and mounted his horse, galloping back to where he had left his group of men.

"We attack now!" he shouted.

His men grabbed their weapons and quickly assembled, their faces hardening with fury.

Rexus dismounted and felt for the small mirror in his pocket, the same one each of the leaders of the other groups carried. He turned his mirror in the sun, catching the light, reflecting it, the sign they had made that they were ready to attack.

One after another, bright lights twinkled at him from behind houses, until he counted ten. Eleven, including his group, had made it, meaning only one hadn't.

Rexus looked back at his group and nodded, his heart racing wild.

"For freedom!" he yelled as pulled his sword from its sheath and ran into the square, the revolutionaries following at his heels. Although his hands trembled and his throat was dry, he didn't falter in the least. All around him the other groups of revolutionaries dashed out from behind shadows and buildings, their roars filling the square.

Rexus hacked his way through the wall of Empire soldiers, and then past three more inside the square, his eyes glancing at the platform when he wasn't fighting. He needed to get there before it was too late, he knew, before they lost their lives.

"Fight with us and win your freedom!" he yelled to the civilians as he worked his way through the crowd.

Slowly, he noticed that the men around him started to fight the enemy with their bare hands.

Chaos erupted.

Empire soldiers took to attacking the citizens, butchering any and all who were in close proximity. Rexus redoubled his efforts, slashing down soldiers as he went. As his men swarmed the square from all sides, he looked up to see General Draco being ushered away beneath a mountain of shields. Rexus grabbed an arrow from his quiver, aimed it through a narrow gap in the shields, and released.

A moment later, General Draco cried out and fell, and was lying on the platform with an arrow in his shoulder.

The soldiers who had protected him turned toward Rexus.

"Arrest him!" a soldier yelled.

But Rexus was quick as lightning with his bow and he shot them down so swiftly, not one reached him. He dashed toward the poles, and with the help of other revolutionaries, released the prisoners from their shackles, freeing them before it was too late.

But where was Anka? he wondered, glancing around.

There was no time to search. Rexus stood at the edge of the platform and wound his bow, killing as many Empire soldiers as he had arrows.

Finally, the wall of Empire soldiers encircling the plaza broke open on the northern side, and women and children were rushed to the side streets, leaving only men left battling against their persecutors amidst the clanging of swords and groaning of men. Men fell on both sides, piling up in the streets which ran with blood.

Rexus hopped down from the podium, slaying soldier after soldier, fully engrossed in a battle he knew would either make or break the rebellion.

His heart broke a little more each time he saw one of his men or a civilian fall. He worked himself up into such a frenzy that he imagined he might never die at the hands of an Empire sword.

But just then, two soldiers came at him at once, one stabbing him from the side, the other pounding a hammer at him from above.

The blow to the head was sudden—dizzying—the sword in the shoulder a sharp pain that made a shriek tumble from his lips as he fell to the ground.

Momentarily, he could not see. Flailing his sword out in front of him, trying to defend himself, he felt another sharp stab in the leg.

He tried to focus his eyes, everything a blur.

An outcry made him recoil into a fetal position. The echoes of the battle surrounded him.

Now, he thought, now I die.

And with that thought, he knew Ceres would never know how much he cared.

But no sword punctured his chest. No spear was thrust into his abdomen. Instead, he heard grunts as swords collided.

When Rexus was finally able to focus his eyes again, he saw Nesos going at the two Empire soldiers, carrying a sword in one hand, a spear in the other.

Slowly, Rexus rose to his feet, the wound in his shoulder stinging, the blow to his head still making him feel dizzy, and the wound in his leg screaming. He fell over once, but stood straight back up.

Nesos buried his spear in one of the Empire soldier's necks, and feeling his strength return, Rexus sunk his spear deeply into the enemy's armpit.

A horn blared through the plaza, and the Empire soldiers looked up and began to evacuate toward the side streets. Mobs of citizens followed after and killed them.

The revolutionaries cheered, Nesos included. But Rexus couldn't lift his arm and his knees felt suddenly very weak.

Nesos ran toward him, catching him in the fall, helping him onto the ground ever so gently.

As stillness settled at the piazza, Rexus lay there and looked toward the Alva Mountains, toward the cave, the castle, where he knew the bulk of his men were.

His eyes widened. His soul cried.

The castle was engulfed in a fiery inferno.

The revolution was over.

CHAPTER NINETEEN

Ceres's hair stood on the back of her neck as she waited for the axe to descend on her. The crowd had gone silent, and she heard her executioner raise his weapon into the air.

In that moment, her entire life flashed before her.

Yet, to her surprise, the blade never dropped.

Instead, she felt arms around her waist.

And a moment later, someone was hoisting her into the air.

She landed on her stomach, hunching forward, and realized she was draped across a horse's back, her legs on one side, her head on the other. Someone hopped onto the same horse right behind her, whipping it to a sudden start, and Ceres felt a strong arm holding her around her waist, preventing her from falling. She heard arrows swooshing by, hitting against armor or a shield.

The Empire soldiers yelled, the spectators clamored, but their voices slowly vanished as the horse galloped away.

The horse stopped after riding for a while, and she felt her new captor descend the horse. Then sturdy hands grabbed her waist, lifted her off, and set her onto the ground.

She removed the blindfold from her eyes and her breath stopped when she saw Thanos's face.

"Come," he said, taking her hand, pulling her with him toward the palace.

"Wait," she said. "Why...how...?"

She noticed her hands were still shaking, and she couldn't believe she wasn't yet dead.

He dragged her into the main entrance, her knees so wobbly she could barely keep up, confusion and anger and surprise reeling through her at once.

"We must speak to the king and queen this instant before the Empire soldiers hunt us down," Thanos said.

Ceres stiffened and snatched her hand from his, the thought of seeing the king and queen petrifying.

"No! Why?" she asked. "They ordered my execution."

Thanos pulled her behind a pillar in the vestibule, gently shoving her against the cold marble, looking into her eyes.

"I meant what I said at the Stade," he said.

She narrowed her eyes.

"You can trust me with your life."

When he leaned forward and rested his forehead against hers, she became breathless.

"And...I need you," he said.

Thanos lifted his hand and looked at Ceres's mouth while tracing her lips with his fingertips, his touch as light as a feather.

She shivered in delight, his scent all around her, his face an inch away, but the war between her head and her heart caused her to stiffen. She should not, no, she would not delight in his touch, she forbade her body. He was still the enemy, and for as long as she lived, he needed to remain that.

Reaching behind her head, he pressed his cheek to hers, the tenderness causing Ceres to let out a faint sigh. She felt his hand wrap around his waist, their bodies pressed against each other, warm, tender.

"But you must tell no one," he said, pulling away. "Come. We need to see the king and queen. I have a plan."

Against her will, she let him lead her into the colossal vestibule, and they ran past massive marble pillars that reached all the way to the high ceiling. Ceres had never seen the likes of such architecture; it seemed the palace was a building made by the gods. Silk curtains, shiny chandeliers, marble statues, and golden vases adorned the interior. Having just been in the dungeon, having lived in extreme poverty her entire life, it was as if she had been transported into another world.

Arriving at the second floor, he led her to an enormous bronze door and opened it. They stepped into a huge rectangular room, and at the end of red marble pillars, and rows of seats filled with finely dressed men and women, were two thrones. There sat the king and queen.

Holding Ceres's hand, Thanos walked toward the thrones.

The king rose, his face red, blood vessels protruding from his forehead.

"What have you done?" he bellowed.

The queen placed a hand on the king's, but the king only returned her gesture with a threatening glare.

"If you promise to spare Ceres's life, I will agree to marry Stephania," he announced.

Ceres glanced at Thanos sideways, wondering what he was doing, confused about his earlier advance.

"Do you think you run this kingdom, boy?" the king said, and then turned to the Empire soldiers. "Arrest them!"

"You will not arrest me!" Thanos yelled, taking a bold step forward as he pointed at the king.

But the Empire soldiers did not heed Thanos.

The king waved his hand and with that, Ceres and Thanos were grabbed again, and this time, both were hauled off to the dungeon.

*

Ceres stood by the bars, peering out into the dungeon hallway, her disbelief slowly being replaced with hopelessness. It hadn't even been an hour, and here she was again in this rotting hole, awaiting her fate. At least now they had the cell to themselves, no thugs to fear, but other than that, she knew her circumstances were bleak. Extremely bleak.

She thought of the others she had been brought to the scaffolding with, wondering if their sentence had been completed, if they were now one of thousands of casualties at the hands of the cruel Empire.

And then there was Apollo... Tears filled her eyes and she whisked one away as it fell.

She glanced over at Thanos sitting on the filthy floor, his dignity stripped with one word from the nasty king.

"I'm sorry," he said, leaning his head backward onto the dungeon wall. "I didn't think my uncle would throw us in prison."

"You couldn't have known," Ceres said.

"I should have."

There was a long pause, for what was there to say? Ceres wondered. Examining the events that had led them here wouldn't change their circumstances.

Thanos stood up and paced back and forth a few times.

"I misjudged the queen's desire to have me marry Stephania," he said.

He kicked the wall several times and rattled the cage so hard Ceres thought he might break the bars.

"Don't blame yourself for others' cruelty," she said once he had calmed down, their eyes connecting in the dimness.

"I should have never stopped that horse."

She held his eyes, his stare intense, the memory of his fingertips on her mouth and of his body pressed against hers still resonating through her.

She heard footsteps coming down the passageway, and when she turned, she saw numerous Empire soldiers throw a young lady and several men into the cell next to them.

She gasped.

"Anka?" she said as she peered through the iron bars, recognizing her.

Anka clamped bloodied hands around the bars, her body covered in burn marks, her lovely black locks gone, shorn in uneven lengths.

"Ceres?" she said, her eyes popping.

The Empire soldiers opened the door to Ceres's cell and pulled Thanos and Ceres out, dragging them down the hallway.

"What happened? Are my brothers well? Is Rexus?" Ceres yelled back at Anka, desperate to know the answers.

"There was a battle…" Anka started.

But they turned the corner, and Ceres could no longer hear Anka's voice over the thrashing of the Empire soldiers' heavy boots. It crushed her.

"I demand you tell me where you are taking us," Thanos said.

The soldiers remained silent and pushed them forward, and Ceres's heart was racing the way it did when she was on her way to her execution.

Down the hallway they were shoved, and once they arrived at the staircase, the Empire soldiers stopped.

"Go," one said.

Perplexed, Ceres looked to Thanos. He took her hand, and together they started to climb the stairs.

What would await them at the top? Ceres wondered, finding it impossible to believe or hope she truly was free to go. Was there a wagon standing there to take them to the scaffolding? Were a dozen Empire soldiers standing in wait, ready to shoot them down with flaming arrows?

Thanos squeezed her hand, his face appearing much calmer than the raging anxiety she felt inside, and she wondered how he could be calm at such a moment as this.

Arriving at the top of the steps, Ceres saw the queen standing in front of them, her hands clasped in front of her body.

The queen glanced down at Ceres's and Thanos's joined hands and frowned.

"I spoke some sense into the king and he agreed to set you free so long as you solemnly swear to wed Stephania," she said.

"I swear it," Thanos said, tightening his grip around Ceres's hand.

"And with that, I expect you two to cease any and all contact other than when you are training for the Killings," the queen said, her eyes narrowing into slivers.

"Understood," Thanos said with a nod.

The queen stepped forward and locked cold eyes on Ceres.

"As for you, little girl," she said, "I have plans for you, and you might think you are glad to keep your life, but soon you will regret that you weren't beheaded on that scaffolding today."

The queen turned on her heels and marched away, Ceres now realizing it was quite possibly even deadlier inside the castle walls than out.

CHAPTER TWENTY

Ceres arrived extra early the next morning at the palace training grounds, her mind still reeling from the events of the night before, from how close she had come to death. And most of all, from thoughts of Thanos. She owed him her life. And yet she did not know if she loved or hated him. And knowing Rexus was out there, waiting for her, she hated feeling this way about anyone else.

Anxious to take her mind off of all this and resume training with Thanos, Ceres focused on her work. With great care, she laid out the weapons she thought he might use in today's practice, and then she filled the drinking bucket with fresh water.

She was focusing when suddenly, out of the corner of her eye, she saw Lucious walking straight toward her, his eyes filled with loathing, his muscles rigid with aggression. She tensed. Not a single other person was in sight, and now she wished she had not been so early.

And then, when she saw *her* sword in Lucious's hand, her heart started to race.

She knew she couldn't fight him—he might have her arrested and thrown in prison again. But she couldn't not defend herself either, knowing he would have no qualms about killing her.

Then a thought popped into her mind. Had the queen set this up?

Alarmed, she glanced around to see if anyone else might be on their way, but she heard no voices and saw no one in the distance.

Approaching, Lucious scowled and took a threatening step in her direction, his hand squeezing the hilt, the blood vessels in his forehead protruding.

"Place the sword on the table!" Ceres heard a deep voice growl behind her.

She swiveled around and saw a stranger. He was dressed in the manner of the southern isles, his longer than usual tunic similar to those she had seen from those parts. His skin was golden, his shoulder-length black hair kept in a ponytail, and his posture was an erect board.

With dark, slanted eyes, he glared at Lucious with such intensity, Ceres was convinced the stranger could kill with his eyes alone.

Lucious pinched his lips together and laid her sword onto the weapon table.

"Now leave," the man said.

Lucious gave him a disapproving look, but did as the stranger said and stomped off with a huff.

"I take it you are Ceres?" the man asked.

She hesitated to answer, wondering if this man could be trusted. Perhaps he was an assassin sent to kill her by the queen, the queen's words bouncing around inside of her skull.

"Who are you?" she asked.

"You may call me Master Isel," the man said. "I am your new fighting master."

At first, she thought she had misheard him, especially when she considered the queen's last comment to her. But the way Isel looked at her, with respect and dignity in his eyes, she almost dared to believe what he had said was true.

"From now on, for three hours a day, I will train you to become a combatlord," he said. "I will instruct you like a man, so no man can ever touch you or triumph over you. Do you accept?"

Now she believed it was true, but why? And it surprised her that he even asked that question. Was *not* accepting an option? She knew even if it were, she would be a fool to decline.

"What is the purpose of this training?" she asked.

"Thanos sent me to you. A gift to make you strong. To give you what you so craved: a chance to learn to fight. To truly fight."

A shrill of joy erupted in her chest, and for a moment she couldn't breathe.

"Do you accept, or do I need to tell him that you so respectfully declined?" he asked, a twinkle in his eye.

"I accept. I accept," she said.

"Well then. If you are ready, let us begin."

She nodded and turned toward her sword to pick it up.

"No!" Isel said.

Startled, Ceres swiveled around.

"First, you must learn how to die."

Puzzled, Ceres squinted her eyes.

"Stand in the center of the practice arena," he said, pointing his sword toward it.

Ceres followed his instructions, and once she had taken her place, he walked a slow circle around her.

"Royal combatlords are expected to behave a certain way," he said. "When you represent the king, the Empire, a standard of excellence is required of you."

She nodded.

"There are specific death rituals, and you are expected to die bravely, with no trace of fear, offering yourself to cold-blooded murder."

"I understand," she said.

He faced her, his hands clasped behind his back.

"I see a lot of fear in your eyes," he said. "Your first lesson is to eradicate any traces of vulnerability, of gentleness, and most importantly, of fear from your countenance."

He stepped closer.

"Your mind is on other things, in other places. When you are with me, no *one* and no *thing* else exists anywhere!" he yelled with passion in his voice.

"Yes, Master Isel."

"To be a contender, as a girl, you must work twice as hard, three times as hard as the men, and if they sense any weakness in you, they will use it against you."

She nodded, knowing he spoke the truth.

"Your second lesson starts right away, and it is a lesson in strength. You are skinny. You need more muscle," he said. "Come."

She followed Isel down to the ocean side and he stopped at the jutting cliffs.

For the first two hours, he had her lift heavy boulders, throw heavy rocks, and climb the steep cliff.

Just when her body begged for her to be done, for the last hour, he compelled her to performed sequences of sprints and push-ups across the sand.

By the end of Ceres's lesson, her clothes were completely drenched with sweat and her muscles trembled from fatigue, and she could scarcely manage to walk back up to the palace where the other warriors were sparring.

At the top, Master Isel handed her a wooden cup.

"You will drink this every day," he said. "It is a tonic of ashes—good for strong bones."

She gulped the foul-tasting drink down, her arms so exhausted she could barely bring the cup to her lips.

"Tomorrow, I will meet you here at dawn to continue your strength training and more," he said.

Master Isel nodded toward a hefty blonde handmaiden, and the happy girl approached.

"Until tomorrow, Ceres," he said, walking away into the gardens.

"Please follow me, my lady," the handmaiden said and started toward the palace.

Ceres didn't think she could walk another step, but somehow, when she told her legs to move, she managed to follow.

The handmaiden led her into the palace, up four sets of stairs, and toward the western tower. Up at the very top of a spiraling staircase, they walked into a room. The bed sheets were made of silk, the drapes of fine linen, and a bed as wide as it was long stood against the northern wall.

Four dresses were laid out on the bed, two made of the finest silk, and two of soft linen. In front of the fireplace, on top of a white fur rug, stood a tub filed with steaming water, iris petals floating on the surface.

"Master Isel had this food ordered especially for you, my lady," the handmaiden said.

Her stomach growled when she saw a table covered in meats, fruits, vegetables, barley, beans, and breads. She walked over to it and devoured several mouthfuls of food, washing it down with wine from a golden goblet.

"May I help you undress for the bath, my lady?" the handmaiden asked after Ceres had finished eating.

Ceres felt a sudden rush of shyness come over her. Have someone undress her?

"I…" she balked.

But before she could decline, the handmaiden was tugging the shirt out of Ceres's pants, and once she was fully undressed, the handmaiden helped Ceres into the tub, the hot water enveloping her, soothing every sore muscle.

The girl proceeded to wash Ceres's skin with a sponge, and next, she worked on Ceres's hair, detangling it with a sweet-smelling honeysuckle conditioner, turning Ceres's hair as smooth as silk.

She climbed out of the tub, and the handmaiden dried her off, after which she rubbed oil into Ceres's skin. Then the girl applied makeup to Ceres's face.

"Your dress, my lady," the handmaiden said, holding up the coral-colored one.

First, she helped Ceres into a white tunic that reached her ankles and covered her shoulders, and then she dressed her in the coral dress, securing it with a golden brooch above each shoulder.

Studying the material, Ceres saw that the fabric was embroidered with golden thread, the pattern reminding her of lilies of the valley.

Finally, the handmaiden braided Ceres's hair into a partial up-do, and on her head, she placed a thin golden headband in the shape of a wreath.

"You are lovely, if I might say so, my lady," the handmaiden said with a smile as she stood back, admiring Ceres.

There was a subtle knock at the door, and the handmaiden answered it.

Ceres looked at herself in the mirror, hardly recognizing herself, her lips stained red, her face dusted with chalk, her eyes darkened with eye makeup. Although she was grateful for the food and the warm bath, she loathed how she looked like the princesses, the very ones she had her entire life hated.

Then she had an idea and turned toward the messenger at the door.

"Will you please tell Thanos I wish to have Anka, the girl who is in prison, for my handmaiden?" Ceres asked.

The messenger bowed.

"I will relay the message," he said.

The handmaiden closed the door and walked over to where Ceres stood.

"An invitation for you, my lady," she said with a bow.

Ceres picked the note off the silver platter and unrolled it.

Ceres,

If it pleases you, I would love the honor of your company this afternoon. It would be my greatest joy if you would meet me at the library.

Sincerely,
Thanos

Ceres sat down on the bed and tried to ignore the excitement that hummed through her at the thought of seeing Thanos again—just the two of them—at the library, of all places. She loved to study, and had frequently snuck away from home to read scrolls at the library just twenty minutes from her parents' house.

I mustn't feel excited at the thought of seeing Thanos, she commanded herself, the note dropping to her side. If she allowed her affection for him to grow, deceiving him, and then betraying him, would be so very hard to do. And she loved Rexus. How could she even consider such an invitation from the enemy they a few days ago jointly despised?

Accepting Thanos's invitation was dangerous, too, Ceres knew. Just yesterday the queen had ordered they not see each other outside of practice, and here Thanos was openly defying her command. Had he no fear?

It didn't seem so.

Had he really agreed to marry Stephania to save her life? Ceres marveled. It was the kindest thing anyone had done for her. Too kind, in fact.

She should tell him it was too much of a sacrifice.

Yes, that was what she would do: accept his invitation and tell him, after which she would remind him that he had agreed not to see her.

CHAPTER TWENTY ONE

This will not end well, Ceres thought as she walked down the winding staircase from her room, her handmaiden leading the way. With sweaty hands, and a heart that refused to beat at a reasonable pace, every few seconds, she'd stop and almost turn back to her chamber. There, it was safe. There, Thanos wouldn't visit her, and she wouldn't hate herself for accepting his invitation and for being untrue to Rexus.

She stopped at the bottom of the stairwell and peered down the hallway at the dozens of marble columns that lined the passage, the handmaiden continuing on. The ceilings seemed as high as mountaintops, the floor smooth as a lake on a quiet day, and the mural paintings covering the walls depicted former kings, queens, beasts, and nature.

The handmaiden, now several feet in front of Ceres, turned around and waved.

"Well, come on then," she said. "Or perhaps you are too sore?"

She was sore, yes, but that wasn't the reason she wasn't moving. However, she knew she needed to do this so she pulled her shoulders back, took a deep breath, and strode forward.

Once downstairs, the handmaiden led Ceres outside and walked her through the courtyard and to the side of the palace.

They arrived at a separate building, the face of the library having six marble columns. In front was a small fountain with a statue of the queen at the top, the queen's steely gaze looking down at Ceres.

Even here she is watching, Ceres thought.

"Is there anything else I can do for you before I leave?" the handmaiden said with a smile.

Ceres shook her head and watched as the girl sauntered off.

"Ceres?" she heard behind her.

She turned to see Thanos standing there, a white toga draped around his body, his dark curls combed back neatly. Although more formal-looking than usual, it was a good look for him, Ceres observed. She tried not to like it too much.

"I almost didn't recognize you," he said.

"I look...not like me," she said, twisting her hands into knots.

"You look exactly like you, just a little cleaner," he said, the slightest look of amusement in his face.

He leaned in and inhaled.

"And you smell good," he said.

Of all things to notice, she thought, irritated, though she couldn't stop her heart from beating a little faster.

"Did I not before?" she asked, raising an eyebrow.

"Not as much as a girl," he said.

"Well, don't get used to it. In the arena, I'll still *not* smell like a girl."

He laughed heartily, and that made Ceres even more irritated at him.

"Shall we?" he asked, holding his arm out for her to take it.

Without taking his arm, she walked right past him and up the stairs toward the library. She heard him exhaling sharply behind her.

Stepping inside, Ceres gasped when she saw thousands upon thousands of scrolls stacked into wooden shelves on every wall. She had never seen so many writings in one place—the other library she had studied at was much smaller. Oh, how she would love to sit in this room for days and weeks and months and soak up all the knowledge that was in here.

The room was hot, the scent of wood and parchment inundating the musty air, and on the sides, by wooden tables, in between marble pillars, sat scholars dressed in togas, writing. There was a hushed reverence, and Ceres felt giddy to be here.

In the center of the library an elderly man stood at a marble slab, hunched over a scroll as he read. His head was bald, making his large ears more pronounced, and he had penetrating blue eyes that sat over a long, beaky nose.

He looked up and smiled, and immediately, Ceres knew she would like him.

Thanos walked in behind her and placed his hand on the small of her back, heat collecting there as he gently pushed her forward toward the old man.

"Ceres, meet Cosmas," Thanos said. "He is the royal scholar, among other things."

"I am honored to meet you," Ceres said with a nod and a slight curtsy.

"The honor is mine, my dear," the old man replied, his smile widening as he took her hand.

"What other sorts of things?" Ceres asked.

Thanos rested a hand on Cosmas's shoulder, his eyes filled with tenderness.

"Counselor, teacher, friend, father," he said.

The old man gasped a laugh and nodded.

"Father, yes."

Cosmas rolled up the scroll in front of him, but even though Ceres itched to know what was written on it, she didn't quite dare to ask to read it, thinking it might not be acceptable.

"You would never have known it, but you should have seen Thanos when he arrived at the castle," he said in a voice that sounded like it might crack any second. "He was such a scrawny little thing, one would never have thought he would grow up to look like a god."

Ceres laughed. Thanos stepped behind the old man and tapped his ear. Ceres nodded, realizing the man was hard of hearing.

"Thanos may have told you, but he lost his parents when he was but a babe. Such nice folks they were," Cosmas said, shaking his head, his lips tilting downward.

"I'm sorry to hear," Ceres said, glancing at Thanos, but Thanos said nothing.

The old man picked up the scroll, but before he could put it away, curiosity overcame Ceres, and she pushed her hesitation aside.

"May I read it?" she asked, forcing her voice to be louder than usual so Cosmas would hear her.

Thanos's eyes widened, and he had a look of disbelief on his face.

"What?" Ceres asked, feeling a little embarrassed from his stare.

"I guess…I just assumed you couldn't read," he said.

"Well, you assumed wrong," she retorted. "I love studying everything I can get my hands on."

Cosmas laughed and winked at her.

"Although this isn't the largest library in Delos, it is the oldest and carries the writings of the greatest philosophers and some of the best scholars in the world," Cosmas said. "You are more than welcome to study anything in here."

"Thank you," Ceres said, letting her eyes scan the scrolls. "I could live in this place."

"Hold on," Thanos said, his eyes narrowing, his expression filled with skepticism. "What is it you have you studied, exactly?"

"Mathematics, astronomy, physics, geometry, geography, physiology, and medicine, among other things," Ceres said.

Thanos nodded, a look of wonder, and perhaps even a look of pride in his eyes, Ceres saw.

"Thanos, why don't you give the dear a tour of the rest of the library, and we can study when you return?" Cosmas said.

"Would you like to see it?" Thanos asked.

"Of course," Ceres replied, bubbles of excitement rising within at the thought.

Thanos offered his arm again, but just like before, she sauntered right past him, not taking it. He rolled his eyes.

First Thanos took her to the study room, then a lecture hall and a meeting room, before finally showing her out to the library gardens.

They walked in silence on the stone path, past statues of gods and goddesses, manicured bushes, vine-covered pillars, and endless beds of brightly colored flowers. A gentle breeze delighted her face, the scent of roses stirring into the air.

At the back of her mind, she remembered there was something she had planned to say to Thanos, but with him here, she couldn't seem to recall what it was.

"I must admit, I was quite shocked when you started to list off all the philosophies you had studied," Thanos said. "I'm sorry I didn't believe you at first."

"Well, in your defense, most commoners aren't schooled, and most royals think they know everything about everyone, so how could you have known?" she said.

He chuckled at the jibe.

"I'll be the first to admit I am ignorant in many things," he said.

She glanced at him sideways. Was he pretending to be humble? She couldn't tell.

"How did you become learned?" he asked, clasping his hands behind his back as he walked.

"My father's best friend was a scholar, and the scholar would let me sneak into the library and read. And more often than not he would even sit down with me and teach me," she said.

"I'm glad there are some reasonable men out there, encouraging women to study," he said.

Ceres glanced at him again, trying to assess if he were being genuine in his remark or not, thinking he couldn't possibly be.

"Cosmas is one of those men. If you would like, I could have him continue to tutor you."

Ceres was unable to repress an ear-to-ear smile.

"I would like that. I would love that," she said.

They walked on a while longer until they came to a half-circle of marble pillars. Thanos bid her to sit on the stone bench, and after she sat down, he sat next to her. When she saw the city and the sea beyond, she sighed, for it was so beautiful.

"I didn't realize your parents died when you were young," Ceres said.

He looked out across the city, his nose wrinkling slightly.

"I don't remember them, although I have heard quite a few stories about them from Cosmas."

He paused and pressed a hand next to hers, resting on the bench, their pinky fingers touching.

She couldn't help but notice how her stomach fluttered.

"I do often wonder what they were like, and especially what it would be like to have the love of a mother," he said.

"How did they die?" she asked, her voice soft.

"It's uncertain, but Cosmas thinks someone murdered them."

"How horrible!" Ceres exclaimed, placing her hand atop his without thinking.

Realizing what she had done, she was about to pull her hand away, but Thanos grabbed it before she could and held it tight.

They sat like that for a moment that seemed to span eternity, hearts beating strong, breaths ceased.

She would not look into his eyes, she told herself, for she knew if she did, something would happen. Something terrible. Something wonderful.

He placed a hand underneath her chin and lifted it so she had no other place to look but into his eyes.

And all of a sudden it was as if all the air had vanished from around her and she felt warm, warmer than she had ever felt.

His dark eyes flicked to her lips, and some unseen force drew her to him, pulling her away from her resolve to stay away, pulling her away from Rexus and all she had ever held dear.

With a soft smile, he lifted a hand and stroked her cheek, and Ceres could not for the life of her look away. He leaned forward, his lips finding her throat, so soft.

She took in a staggered breath while her hands knitted through his thick dark curls. She found his lips, warm, soft, and she moved hers across his, slowly, tingles spreading through her, and all that had ever been and all that was, was no more.

"Thanos!" Ceres heard, a female voice, bringing her back to reality.

She turned her head to see Stephania standing there, her lips pinched together tightly, tears in her eyes.

Thanos gave Stephania a hard glare.

"The king needs to see you," Stephania snapped.

"Can't it wait?" Thanos asked.

"No, it is of an urgent matter," Stephania said.

Thanos exhaled a slow breath, an expression of disappointment in his eyes. He stood up and bowed toward Ceres.

"Until next time," he said, and marched back toward the library.

Feeling quite embarrassed, Ceres rose to her feet and was about to leave, but Stephania stepped in her way, eyes seething.

"You will stay away from Thanos, you hear? Just because you are dressed as royalty doesn't mean you are one. You have nothing but commoner blood running through your veins."

"I..." Ceres started, but she was interrupted.

"I know Thanos likes you, but soon he will grow tired of you the way he does every commoner. And once you have given him what he wants, he will throw you out of the palace just like he did the other girls."

Ceres didn't believe Stephania for one second.

"If he has so many other girls, why do you want to marry him?" she asked.

"I don't have to explain myself to a lowlife like you. Stay away from my future husband, or I will find a way to make you disappear, do you understand?"

Stephania started back toward the library, but then she turned to face Ceres again.

"And just so you know," she said, "I will be telling the queen about all that I saw."

CHAPTER TWENTY TWO

Thanos paced nervously back and forth outside of Ceres's door, his hands sweaty, his throat dry, his armor too restrictive and hot. Nothing felt right. Nothing *was* right. Although he realized he had no choice other than to accept his uncle's orders, he knew Ceres would not understand and that she would be hurt and quite possibly hate him for it. And the worst part was, she would be in the right to do so. Even he despised himself for agreeing to do as his uncle had commanded, and he wished there was some way out of this nightmare of a predicament.

Thanos wiped the sweat beading on his brow, and cursed silently.

It was idiotic to pace about here like a drunken fool, he knew, for the king had commanded him to leave immediately, so there was no time. But Ceres deserved the truth from him even if it would cause a mountain of a rift between them. Even if his greatest fear came true—that she would never want to see him again.

Never.

He squeezed his eyes shut as the horror of that thought settled in. And then he realized there was another reason he was here. A huge part of him needed to see her again, in the event he was killed.

He shouldn't think of matters he had no control over, he reprimanded himself.

He gritted his teeth and knocked on the door, and once the new handmaiden opened, he stepped inside.

Right when Ceres saw him, her face went pale.

"Thank you for freeing Anka and for allowing me to have her as my handmaiden," Ceres said.

He glanced at the girl and nodded toward Ceres.

"Of course. Ceres, may I have a word?" he asked.

Thanos noted that Ceres's shoulders went tense, and an unsettled look in her eyes verified she knew something was terribly wrong.

"Of course," Ceres said.

"Perhaps we can take a walk," he said.

They went into the hallway and climbed the stairs to the rooftop, a warm breeze tugging at his hair. From here, Thanos could see the entire capital, houses built as if on top of each other, and he could even hear the riots on the streets.

He stopped at the veranda and faced Ceres. She was so beautiful, he thought, her white dress blowing in the wind, her strawberry blonde hair moving with the breeze. But it wasn't her beauty that made him adore her so. It was her thirst for life and learning, and the passion she carried for the people and things she loved.

He took a deep breath and looked her in the eyes before he spoke.

"King Claudius has ordered the royal army to annihilate the rebellion," he said.

Her lips squeezed together ever so slightly, and she turned away from him, looking across the city.

"Was that what the note was about?" she asked.

"Yes."

"And since you are in your armor, I assume you will be one of the ones enacting the king's orders," she said.

He didn't want to say, the words feeling like molasses in his throat.

"I wish I didn't have to, but I have no choice, Ceres," he said.

"One always has a choice."

Her voice was flat, but it was greatly constrained, he could hear, and he knew with certainty all she wanted to do was scream at him.

"How can you say I have a choice? You have no idea what it's like to live beneath the king, his eyes always scrutinizing you, the threat of death always looming around the corner."

"My brothers are out there!" she yelled, tears welling up in her eyes. "My friend Rexus. Will you kill them if you see them? Will you slay the very ones I love?"

His chest filled with a dull ache, seeing her upset, when all he wanted to do was to make her smile and make her feel safe.

"I realize you are angry—" he said.

"Because they are my people!" she shouted. "They are your people, too, Thanos. Can't you see you are fighting for a corrupt king, for oppression? Is that what you really want?"

Clenching his fist, he remained silent.

"You will be fighting against exactly what it is you yourself are trying to escape. Don't you see?" she said.

He knew she was right, but he had to do this or the king would have no qualms about throwing them both back into the dungeon, like he had threatened when Thanos tried to object.

He gripped the railing, clutching until his knuckles turned white.

"I have to do what I don't want to get the things I desire more."

She stood rigid as a board, her beautiful emerald eyes widening, her mouth open in shock.

128

"What more could you possibly want than for your freedom and for the freedom of your people?" she asked.

"You!" he said.

Ceres's eyes turned conflicted and tears welled up in her eyes. She exhaled a breath and gazed downward, wrapping her arms around her waist as if doing so would protect her heart somehow.

"I need to leave now. I just wanted to inform you where I went before I disappeared," he said.

"Don't go. Please," she whispered, her hands falling limp at her sides, tears rolling down her cheeks.

"I'm sorry, Ceres. I have to."

Her face morphed into a dozen shades of sadness and she let out a cry.

"If you do this, I won't ever talk to you again," she said, her voice shaky and not quite certain. "That's…that's a promise!"

He watched her run away, and although Thanos wanted nothing more than to go after her and take her in his arms, kiss her tenderly, he found his feet immovable. He stood quiet for a moment, anger and shame washing through him.

In order to save himself, he was about to give up all that he loved.

CHAPTER TWENTY THREE

Thanos rode toward General Draco, passing tent after tent, passing tens of thousands of Empire soldiers peppering the Alva Mountains, and he did nothing to hide the animosity in his eyes. The despicable general stood for everything that was wrong with the Empire. In fact, he hated the corrupt man just as much as he hated his uncle; perhaps even more. It was rumored, after all, that General Draco was the one who had killed Thanos's parents.

Thanos finally arrived and dismounted his horse and strode across the scorched grass toward the silver-haired general. The middle-aged man stood in front of his tent, his red cape waving in the wind, a bandage wrapped around his muscular shoulder above his armor. He had been wounded yesterday when Blackrock Square had been stormed by the rebellion, Thanos had heard. If only that arrow had pierced his black heart.

"Come, my new lieutenant," General Draco said.

Thanos did not want that title; the king had forced it upon him. And now that the Empire stood between Ceres and him, driving a deep wedge that could destroy any chance he had at being with her, he detested it even more. However, he valued his and Ceres's life, so he would honor the title until the rebellion had been squashed.

Thanos followed the general inside the tent, where they ended standing around the massive oak strategy table in the middle of the room, a map of Delos and figurines strategically placed upon it.

"Your uncle speaks very highly of your combat and strategy skills, Thanos. I hope you will live up to your reputation." The general spoke in a rushed manner.

Thanos said nothing.

"The rebellion has grown out of hand, and we must squelch it today," General Draco said. "The rebels attacked Fountain Square today, as we suspected they would, and at this very moment, Empire soldiers are forcing them out of the piazza, northward. The instant you leave this tent, you will lead a company of one hundred and twenty men to the north side of Fountain Square, to here."

The general pointed to the map.

"You will capture or kill the leaders of the rebellion, and bring them back to camp dead or alive."

Thanos's heart groaned because he knew anyone brought back alive would be tortured to death. It would be more merciful to kill them all, he thought, although he didn't want to do that either.

"This mission must not fail, and due to the king's high recommendation, I requested you for this task," the general said.

"I understand," Thanos said.

"And just in case you need motivation, your uncle told me to inform you, if you do not succeed on this mission, he will have Ceres thrown into the dungeon, and she will be used as bait in the next Killings."

*

With one hundred and twenty Empire soldiers and four wagons of weapons in tow, Thanos arrived about a mile north of Fountain Square, at the very street where the Empire soldiers would steer the rebels. He ordered his men to stack weapons in abandoned houses, set up traps on the streets, and carry the firepots onto the rooftops.

Thanos climbed to the roof with two dozen Empire soldiers, while the others hid inside houses behind closed shutters to wait for the revolutionaries to pass by. He stood there, pacing, waiting, hating himself more with every minute that passed.

Hardly five minutes passed when Thanos heard the first set of horse hooves pounding against the cobblestones. Still fraught with conflict about his mission, detesting how he was being used as a pawn in the king's game, he lit the tip of his arrow and waited for the revolutionaries to come galloping around the corner. He could not rebel outwardly against the king, he knew; and yet he could find a way to do minimal damage to the rebels, and especially to those closest to Ceres.

Within seconds, four men on horses dashed by, their blue ensigns waving in the wind. Before they could pass, they were shot down with arrows from other Empire soldiers, and fell wounded in the street.

Thanos's arrow was still in his bow. Sweat trickled down his cheek.

Quickly, the rebels were snatched up by eight Empire soldiers and thrown into a slaver cart to be taken back to the camp for questioning.

This isn't right, Thanos thought. He knew he had no choice but to slaughter them.

Or did he? Could he save these men and women they were ordered to attack?

A group of nineteen came next, and just as they rode past Thanos, the Empire soldiers on the rooftops tilted the firepots, the hot oil drenching the revolutionaries. Their shrieks pierced

Thanos's heart, and he had to look away from the writhing bodies on the streets. Once the hot oil had cooled, all nineteen were thrown into a slaver cart to be taken back to camp.

Just as the Empire soldiers had finished clearing the streets, hiding the evidence of the attack, another small group of riders came galloping toward them.

"Rexus!" Thanos heard one of the men yell.

Immediately, Thanos remembered Ceres had mentioned that name when they had spoken on the rooftop of the palace, and his gaze scanned the revolutionaries.

A muscular blond man turned his horse around and steered it to the side of the street, waving.

Behind the small group rode a slew of revolutionaries, but before they arrived at the attack site, Thanos killed the flame on his arrow, hopped down from the roof and into an alleyway, lying in wait for Rexus to pass by.

Before Rexus came close enough, a mob of Empire soldiers stormed out from the houses and started slaying the revolutionaries.

Rexus, Thanos could see, startled at the surprise attack, but quicker than eyes could follow, Rexus pulled one arrow after another from his quiver, shooting his enemies down, killing every single one he shot.

Once his arrows had been depleted, Rexus hopped down from his horse and pulled his sword, slicing Empire soldiers down left and right with the speed and precision of a combatlord, Thanos saw.

Thanos dashed out from the alleyway and tore after Rexus, his sword held high, pretending he was going to attack. He wanted to get to the young man before anyone else had a chance to slay him dead.

He snuck up behind Rexus and wrapped an iron arm around his neck, and with a hand clasped around the young man's mouth, Thanos dragged him into the dimness of the alleyway.

But Rexus was strong, and he wrestled out of Thanos's grasp, drawing his sword.

Thanos held his hands out in front of him and dropped his sword to the ground.

"I mean you no harm!" he yelled, retreating deeper into the shadows, hoping Rexus would follow.

Rexus slashed at him with a force that had Thanos hopping backwards, frightened he had made a mistake and that this could be his last hour. Rexus lunged and spun around, whirling like a tornado after Thanos, the sword slicing through the air, making a swooshing sound.

"Ceres told me you were her friend!" Thanos said. "I want to help you!"

Rexus paused for a moment, staying his sword.

"This is a trap," he said.

"No. She was worried about you. She knew I would fight, and she mentioned her brothers. She mentioned you."

Rexus hesitated.

"Stay here and you will not be killed," Thanos said.

"I won't leave my men out there to die!" Rexus growled.

Of course he wouldn't, and Thanos should have known that. But he was doing this on the fly, with no time to plan.

As quick as a flash, Thanos snatched an arrow from his quiver and shot Rexus's sleeve, the arrow wedging into the wall behind Rexus, confining him.

The distraction gave Thanos just enough time to dash behind Rexus and knock him on the head with the hilt of his sword.

Rexus fell to the ground unconscious and Thanos exhaled a breath of relief. He might not be able to save everyone, Thanos knew, but at least he had saved one of Ceres's friends' lives.

Thanos climbed back onto the rooftop and looked down toward the street. Many Empire soldiers had fallen—many more than he thought would. He saw the opportunity to save the revolutionaries, yet to make it look like he had made the best decision for his own men. No one would blame him for retreating if he judged that his men were being butchered, losing sorely.

"Empire soldiers retreat!" he shouted. "Retreat immediately!"

A few of the Empire soldiers looked up with questions in their eyes, but Thanos knew they would follow his orders. Empire soldiers were trained to obey no matter the command.

The soldiers on the rooftops trickled down one after another, heading toward the wagons, and the soldiers battling the revolutionaries in the streets and inside houses retreated toward the wagons while fighting the enemy off.

Seeing his men were safe, Thanos was just about to join them, but then a faint sound behind him caught his attention. He glanced back to see a young revolutionary, a sword in one hand, a spear in the other.

Thanos drew his sword and took a step toward the man.

"I have no desire to harm you," he said.

Screaming, the young man came at Thanos, the tip of the spear pointing straight toward Thanos's heart.

Thanos spun around and hacked the spear out of his opponent's hand. The young man slashed, but missed, and before the young man could withdraw his arm, Thanos had sliced it open.

"I do not wish to kill you!" Thanos said again, taking a cautious step back. "Walk away and you will live."

"Anything from an Empire soldier's mouth is a lie!" the young man said.

The young man cried out and his jaw clenched, and in no time he was back at Thanos, jabbing.

"I know you are Prince Thanos!" the young man said, stabbing toward him.

"Correct. And who are you?" Thanos asked, blocking.

"That I will tell you once I have run my sword through you," the young man said.

"I must warn you, I have yet to lose a duel."

The young man's eyebrows rose, no fear present in his face.

"There must always be a first!" he yelled.

The young man sped toward Thanos, their swords crashing then, a power struggle, blade against blade. Shoving with a roar, Thanos pushed him away, but the young man was at him again. He was powerful, Thanos noticed, rage, anger, and passion for his cause probably fueling his strength.

The young man stabbed toward Thanos, but missed as Thanos swerved out of the way.

Thanos didn't want to kill him, but it would seem the young man would not stop until one of them was dead. In a split second, Thanos decided he would try to outrun him.

However, before Thanos could remove himself from the duel, the young man drove for Thanos's heart, but Thanos shifted so the young man tumbled forward.

And as he did, he fell, the blade ending up buried in his own abdomen instead.

The young man fell to the roof with a grunt, and as he drew the sword out of his stomach, he screamed.

Thanos took a few steps toward his enemy.

"Kill me," the young man said, a tinge of fear in his eyes.

Thanos gazed at the young man for a few moments, a feeling of sadness overwhelming him. He slid his sword back into its sheath and turned to walk away.

"I am dying," the young man grunted.

Thanos felt overwhelmed with sadness for him. He shook his head.

"You are," he said, seeing how grievous the wound was, realizing nothing could be done for him.

"I didn't tell you my name," the boy gasped.

Thanos nodded, waiting.

"Then tell me," he said, "and I shall make sure it is known that you died an honorable death."

"My name," he gasped, "is Nesos."

Thanos stared back in horror. Nesos. Ceres's brother.

And as Nesos fell down, dead, Thanos knew his life would never be the same again.

CHAPTER TWENTY FOUR

When Thanos entered the throne room, he noticed the tension right away, the king screaming at General Draco, the dignitaries arguing in their seats, gnashing teeth, and the queen spewing obscenities to an advisor. Everyone was here, he saw, even the princes and princesses who weren't usually at meetings such as this. And for good reason.

On his way back, Thanos had seen the slaughter. Houses had been burned to the ground, and citizens—men, women, and children—were left butchered in the streets, stray dogs eating at their flesh, crows pecking at bodies. A few poor souls had been nailed to the trees, while others hung from nooses. But so many Empire soldiers had died, too, and the revolutionaries weren't any kinder, torturing, desecrating bodies in vile ways and even dismembering them.

He knew this was not a war he wanted to be a part of. Not now. Not ever.

"The rebellion has grown beyond what anyone imagined it could, and now the few revolutionaries have become a monster, that if not slain soon, will vanquish the Empire," General Draco said, standing in front of the king and queen.

Once Thanos reached the bottom of the stairwell below the thrones, the room slowly grew silent.

The king did not reply to the general, but turned his attention to Thanos.

"I send my nephew out on one assignment," he said. "One measly assignment, and what happens? He fails miserably, embarrassing himself and the entire royal family in less than an hour. What have you to say for yourself, Thanos?"

Thanos pinched his lips together, in an attempt to prevent himself from telling his uncle he had failed on purpose.

"It was not just him," General Draco said. "Many failed. As I told you before, we must call in more soldiers from the north. If not, you will lose more battles and we will have a war on our hands."

Thanos was surprised that General Draco stood by him.

"If we don't keep losing, we won't have to bring in more troops," the king said.

"Perhaps, but it doesn't change the reality that we are bleeding more men than what the rebellion is birthing," General Draco said.

The king thought for a moment, running his fingers through his beard, and Thanos was glad the attention was no longer on him.

"I hesitate to call in the troops from the north. It will be days before they arrive," the king said.

"With all due respect, sire, what else can we do?" General Draco asked.

"Are there any other proposals?" the king asked, an open question to the dignitaries in the room.

"We should poison the wells in the city," one said. "And only supply water to the peaceable citizens."

"That might work, but the revolutionaries would only become angrier," the king said. "Perhaps we can offer a deal, a sign of good will, and that will calm their rage."

"Open the king's food storage vaults. Feed them," another said.

The king paused for a moment before nodding.

"Perhaps," he said. "Any other suggestions?"

"Might I speak a word?" the queen asked, eyes cunningly watching Thanos.

All gazes in the room slid toward her.

The king gestured with a hand, allowing her to speak.

"I propose a union between a commoner and a royal, a nuptial between the people and the Empire," she said.

"What did you have in mind, exactly?" the king asked.

"A marriage between Thanos and Ceres," she said.

Gasps went through the throne room, expressions of horror and disbelief painting the advisors' faces.

Thanos was stunned by the queen's suggestion as well. Of course he would have no qualms about marrying Ceres, but for political purposes and to be a puppet in the king and queen's play? He didn't like that one bit. He didn't want them to defile the one thing that was the most precious in his life.

"I think that is an excellent idea," the king said. "A union between a lowly commoner and a royal. The people will love it."

"Thanos was promised to me!" a girl's voice boomed through the room.

Thanos swiveled around, and way in the back of the room stood Stephania, her body rigid, yet her eyes wounded.

Stephania walked down the hallway toward the thrones.

"You may not approach!" the queen yelled. "Go back to your seat and close your lips for the remainder of this meeting."

Stephania stopped in her tracks and looked at Thanos, her cheeks glistening with tears, he could see.

Not until now did he feel sorry for the princess. He had never wanted to marry her, but even she was just a pawn in a game they could never escape.

Thanos nodded at Stephania and gave her as empathetic a look as he could. Perhaps now she would back away, knowing it was not Thanos's decision to wed someone else. Perhaps it would finally set her free.

Stephania turned around, her feet hesitantly taking steps away from Thanos. Then she sped up and continued out the bronze doors at the end, running, her sobs vanishing as the doors closed behind her.

"I think it will put an end to the feud. At least for now," the king said. "Are you in agreement, Thanos?"

The king stared at Thanos, his eyes intense with power, as if with a warning: if Thanos didn't accept, it would be the dungeon for Ceres and him. The king knew his weakness was Ceres, and Thanos was furious with himself for having been so open about it. He should have hidden his affection for Ceres, should have known the king would sooner or later take what was most precious to him and use it against him.

Here he was again without a choice, and Thanos's heart twisted in defiance when he nodded.

"Then let it immediately be broadcast from every watchtower across the city!" the king bellowed. "And by the gods, let us hope it works."

Thanos stood in shock. He didn't think it would be announced so soon.

"Should we not ask her first?" Thanos said.

A few of the dignitaries chuckled.

"It is not a question, but a command, but if you want to let her know before she finds out some other way, you had better run," the king said.

At once, the bells tolled through the city, signaling a royal announcement, the sound igniting Thanos to take action.

He turned on his heels and ran toward the bronze door at the end, and toward Ceres's chamber, hoping he could tell her before it was too late.

But how could he ask her for marriage when he had just slaughtered her brother?

Would he be able to keep it secret?

CHAPTER TWENTY FIVE

Horrorstruck, Ceres stood by the window in her room overlooking Delos, the skyline filled with putrid black smoke rising from burning homes. Clamors filled with unspeakable pain reached all the way to her tower, and families with little ones rushed by in the street below, their faces obscured by panic.

For the past hour or so, she had done nothing but cry—cry for her people, cry for her friends, cry for her brothers, for they could be dead. And Rexus? It was more than she could bear to think about.

Unable to watch the dreadfulness unfold any longer, she walked over to the bed and sat, but just a moment later, she had to return to the window, thinking if she didn't remain there, she was somehow betraying her people.

This? This was what Thanos was fighting for? She was still as furious with him as she had been when he left. He had somehow gotten to her, weaseled his way into her heart, made her care. She had hoped he was different from all the other greedy, power-hungry royals, but when it came down to it, he was the same, and chose to fight for the inequality and injustice that cursed this land.

There was a knock at the door, and Anka opened it.

To Ceres's surprise, and great irritation, in walked Thanos.

"May I have a word in private?" he asked.

"No you may not," Ceres said, glancing back out the window again.

"Please. It is of utmost importance," he said.

After a few moments of hesitation, Ceres nodded to Anka, and the girl left, closing the door behind her.

Ceres stood immovable beside the window, her gaze still on the street below.

"Ceres," Thanos said.

Unwilling to face him, she kept looking out the window.

"What do you want?" she asked.

"I realize you are upset with me for leaving, and I remember you said you never wanted to talk to me again. But can we for just a few minutes set our differences aside?" he said.

She glanced at him, considering his comment.

"I have something important to discuss with you," he said. "What I have to say may save many lives."

"All right," she said.

She walked over to the chair in front of the fireplace and sat down, and he followed after, taking a seat straight across from her.

She could see he was anxious, his eyes shifting nervously about as if he were carefully considering what to say, but it did nothing to make her less angry with him; she simply couldn't forget that when he had left to fight, it had crushed her and destroyed all trust they had built.

"Well?" she said after he hadn't said anything for a while.

"I need you to listen with an open mind," he said. "And heart."

She stared back.

"I just came from a meeting with the king and queen, and they believe there is a way to end all the fighting."

Now her interest was piqued, although her guard was still very much up.

"They suggested a marriage between a commoner and a royal," he said.

Ceres nodded.

"I can see where that might work," she said.

Thanos's shoulders relaxed a little and his face lit up.

"You do?"

"If there is a union between the common people and a royal, perhaps the people will think there will be a change."

Ceres looked him in the eyes, and even though she was as livid with him as she had ever been with anyone, and wanted to wring his neck in a fist fight, she also wanted to be closer to him, for him to close the distance between them and kiss her on the neck the way he had before.

She looked away. Those thoughts, those feelings—she would quash them with every fiber of her being until she could no longer remember them ever being there.

"Did they have anyone in mind?" she asked, thinking perhaps Anka since she had just come from the rebellion.

"Yes," he said.

He stood up and strode two steps, vanquishing the distance between them. He knelt down before her, and it puzzled her why he would do such a silly thing.

"I have something for you," he said.

From a small leather pouch hanging around his waist he pulled out a golden bracelet with a charm in the shape of a swan. Handing it to her, he smiled softly.

"It was my mother's," he said.

Even with how mad she was, she didn't want to offend him and refuse the gift he had just offered her—it was probably the most valuable thing he owned. But did he expect her to forgive him because he gave her a present? How shallow did he think she was? How easily did he think she would forsake her principles? She would not be bought, not ever.

She opened her mouth to speak, but he spoke first.

"Ceres, it is you and I they suggested."

She stared back, floored.

"I would be honored to have your hand in marriage," he added.

She couldn't speak, for suddenly there was a lump in her throat. She would not cry, no, she would not. He might think her tears happy, when all they were, were tears of sadness and resentment, of lost trust and lost friendship. There was no way she could say yes, she knew.

She thought of Rexus, fighting for freedom, risking his life day in and day out in hopes of offering liberty to all. Thanos, he fought against all that, and she could not love someone or marry someone like him. And here Thanos was proposing to her because the king thought it would lull the citizens into believing it might lead to equality. She knew it would not.

"It is not under ideal circumstances, but you have to know, before they suggested it, I had already fallen for you," he said. "I meant what I said on the roof. More than anything, I want you."

She looked away, still hurt and unable to open her heart to forgive.

"I went out to fight, Ceres, but when I did, I couldn't get myself to kill the revolutionaries."

She glanced at him, the news melting some of her anger away.

"I saw Rexus. I pulled him into the alleyway with me and knocked him on the head so he wouldn't be killed by the Empire soldiers," Thanos said.

"Truly?" she asked.

He nodded.

"But there's more."

Ceres nodded, now willing to listen, now feeling ashamed she had been so hard on him.

"I saw your brother Nesos."

She reached for his hand and he took it.

"You did?" she asked, hope filling her chest.

"We fought on the roof top. I didn't know it was him. I didn't…"

"What happened?" she asked.

Thanos paused, and looked up at her with tears in his eyes, and she knew. She knew that look, the look of holding dreadful information from a loved one. The look of pain before it had been shared.

"He fell onto his sword and it stabbed him in the abdomen. I told him I didn't want to hurt him, but he—"

She shot to her feet so fast, the chair behind her screeched across the floor. There was simply nowhere to put the pain that was overpowering her, nowhere to contain something so mighty, nowhere to hide it or store it. It was everywhere all at once.

"MURDERER!" she shrieked, unable to stop herself from crying. "MY BROTHER!"

He stood there, looking dazed.

"I hate you, and abhor everything you stand for!" she yelled.

His eyes flinched, and he exhaled a defeated breath, the hand holding the bracelet falling into his lap.

"Now get out!" she said.

"Ceres, please don't do this," he pleaded.

"Get out!" she yelled. "I said I never wanted to see you again, and I meant it!"

Her chest tightened, her throat clenched shut. She had fallen for him, too, but her heart was foolish, she knew, and this more than anything proved it.

He rose to his feet and stood still for a moment, sorrow canvassing his face.

"I'm sorry, Ceres."

He walked away, leaving the door open behind him.

She turned to the window and wept. Nesos. Her brother. Gone forever. She could hardly breathe with grief.

Hardly had she caught her breath when she heard a sound behind her. She spun, assuming Thanos had returned, preparing to shout at him to leave—but was shocked at who she saw.

The queen.

She stared back haughtily, an evil grin upon her face.

"Hello, Ceres," the queen said, walking into the doorway, eyes rumbling with menace. "How did the proposal go?"

She grinned, stepping closer.

"As Thanos's future bride, your life belongs to the monarchy. It is my responsibility as your queen to see that you are protected. For starters, you will not leave this room unless you are permitted, and for now, I forbid it."

The queen suddenly turned, walked out, and slammed the door shut. Ceres heard a key being thrust into the keyhole.

Enraged, she ran to it and wrapped frantic hands around the door handle, pulling on it with all her might.

But it was too late. The door had been locked, and there was nothing to do but give up, she realized.

She fell to her knees with uncontrollable sobs, slamming her fists on the heavy oak, Nesos's name spilling from her lips.

And yet, amidst her cries, unbeknownst to her, she sometimes confused his name with Thanos's.

.

CHAPTER TWENTY SIX

Ceres didn't know exactly how long she had been sitting on the stone floor in her chamber—it could have been minutes, or hours—tear after tear trailing down her face. It was eerily quiet outside, the riots having ceased. Likely, the news of her and Thanos's marriage announcement was pacifying the leaders of the rebellion. She doubted it would last long.

Oh, how she wished she hated Thanos; and yet her heart was a villain, betraying everything she ever held dear. Sadness overwhelmed her, and she tucked her knees into her chest and sobbed quietly for a moment.

This is what I deserve, she thought as she sat up straight and wiped the wetness from her cheeks, staining the silk sleeves. She hadn't played her cards well, she realized, in this royal game of power and intrigue. And it was becoming clear that if she were to remain at the palace and marry Thanos, she would have to learn how to beat the royals at their own game.

Had she made the right choice in rejecting Thanos? She thought she had, but why then, whenever she thought about his forlorn face when she had rejected him, did it feel as if everything was wrong?

On the other side of the door, keys rattled, and then someone inserted a key into the keyhole. Expecting the queen or an Empire soldier, she scuttled away from the door on hands and knees and dried her tears.

When the door opened, Anka stood in the doorway. She strode into the room and shut the door behind her.

Ceres hopped to her feet, a feeling of elation rushing through her. She ran to Anka and threw arms around her, squeezing tightly.

"You need to get out of here before we are discovered," Anka said. "Go seek out Rexus. The rebellion's new headquarters are down by fisherman's bay, inside Harbor Cave."

Ceres knew the cave well, having played there many times with her brothers growing up. She looked at Anka, so small and lovely, and she could not bear to leave her friend here alone amidst the wolves.

"Come with me," Ceres said, grabbing her hand.

"I cannot. I must stay here until my mission is complete," Anka said. "But here, take this."

Anka slipped her gray hooded cape off and draped it around Ceres's shoulders.

"How will I ever repay you?" Ceres said, embracing Anka again.

"You owe me nothing," Anka said with a smile.

Ceres nodded, remembering speaking those exact words when she rescued Anka from the slaver cart.

"On second thought," Anka said with a smirk, "join the rebellion and make them pay for every person that was ever forced into slavery."

"I will," Ceres said.

Just before Ceres left, she snatched her sword from beneath the bed and fastened the scabbard around her waist. She drew the hood over her head and darted down the stairwell, thrilled to finally be joining the rebellion from within, to stand beside Rexus in the fight for liberty.

She ran down the corridor, eyes peeled, ears alert, her heart galloping. She knew exactly where the guards stood watch, and as she maneuvered through the palace, she made sure to avoid those areas. Moving swiftly, quietly, and above all, in the shadows, she made herself invisible. She reached the kitchen and weaved through boxes of food and past cooks and servants busily working on the royals' next meal.

Stepping into the courtyard, she slunk behind crates of wine and carts of food, passing slaves and Empire soldiers who had their attention elsewhere.

Just as she exited the side gates, she saw an Empire soldier holding up a scroll, speaking from the platform right in front of the palace, dozens of citizens huddling around.

"It has been declared that Prince Thanos will marry the commoner, Ceres. Due to this union, King Claudius and the rebellion have agreed upon a truce. All citizens are hereby commanded to cease and desist any and all opposition to the Empire, which includes…"

His voice faded as she skirted around the corner of a building.

For a few moments, Ceres became breathless, paralyzed, her heart pounding in her throat. The marriage was being publicly announced even though she hadn't agreed to it.

Ceres ran as fast as she could, sprinting down the street. Panting, lungs on fire, she flew by carnage and wreckage southward toward the ocean, the breeze streaming against her body. She cautiously followed the back roads leading to the bay.

The rocky shore was difficult to maneuver, but Ceres dashed as fast as she could towards Rexus's cave. On she ran, hopping over large boulders, stepping on small stones, the sun a globe of fire on her head, causing her to sweat. Even when her legs demanded she stop, and her mouth became parched, she continued on past fishermen and boats, the seagulls above soaring against the blue sky.

I will rest once I am at the cave, she told herself, and with every stride, the excitement in her bosom grew. So much had changed since she had last seen Rexus, and even though it had only been days, it felt as if it had been months. Would things be the same? She needed to share her mourning of her brother with someone, someone who would understand.

By the time she reached the cave the sun had started to set, and the cavern in the mountainside was a gaping black hole behind warped vines and slimy mosses. Other than a handful of scouts hiding on the cliffs and behind bushes, watching her, the outside looked abandoned.

Ceres found herself stopped by flaming arrows shot to the ground right before her feet. She looked up, irritated that they didn't recognize her.

"I am here for Rexus. Nesos and Sartes are my brothers! I am with the rebellion!" she yelled.

Two watchers climbed down from the mountainside, bows strung with arrows, approaching Ceres.

"I must search you for weapons," one said.

"I have a sword, but you will not take it from me," she insisted, opening up the cape, revealing her father's sword.

"Then you will not be allowed inside," he said.

Had they not heard her?

"My name is Ceres and my brothers, Nesos and Sartes, are with the   rebellion," she said with an irritated voice. "I am with the rebellion. Rexus sent me on a mission to the palace and I am here to report. Go ask him. He will vouch for me."

"You're the girl who is supposed to marry Prince Thanos," the other watcher said, mockingly.

She didn't want to waste time explaining to them that, no, she wasn't going to marry Thanos and that she had refused him. Rexus would vouch for her once she was inside.

"Go tell Rexus I am here to report," she said, her voice stern.

One of the watchers headed inside, while the other held her at arrow-point. After a few minutes, the watcher returned.

"Rexus will not see you. He told me to tell you to go marry your prince charming, and to stay away from the rebellion," he said.

She gasped, bursts of pain, but also wrath clenching inside. He would not see her? He thought she had agreed to marry Prince Thanos?

"I demand to see him at once!" she shouted, her body rigid.

"Get lost," one of the watchers said, nudging her with the tip of his arrow.

Ceres realized standing here and arguing would not make one difference.

She spun around, clipping one of the watcher's feet from underneath him so he fell to the rocks with a thud, and before the other watcher could react, she had already drawn her sword and knocked him unconscious with her hilt.

With not a second to waste, arrows raining down at her, she sprinted into the cave. She zoomed by dark, glistening walls, her eyes on the lit torches in the distance, her hands fumbling to get her sword back into its sheath.

"Stop!"

Yells came from behind her, but she would not stop. She would see Rexus, and as soon as she would be given a chance to explain, he would understand that she loved him, and she would know she loved him too. More than Thanos. More than anyone.

"Rexus!" she yelled, slipping on the slimy rocks.

She reached the end of the narrowing, and when she stepped into the larger space, hundreds of eyes were on her, menacing expressions causing her to want to shrink.

"Seize her!" someone yelled.

"I need to speak with Rexus!" she yelled.

A mob of men gathered around her, grabbing her arms. One took her sword and it vanished into the crowd of men and women.

"Rexus!" she yelled.

The mob opened up, and Rexus was standing there before her, his blond hair gleaming in the light of the torches. He looked so forlorn, Ceres thought.

"Rexus," she said, tears in her eyes.

She wrestled free from her captors and threw herself against his firm chest, embracing him so tightly, he grunted.

After a few moments, she noticed his arms were still by his side, limp, not embracing her in return. She pulled back a little and looked up into his gorgeous face. It was as hard and cold as ice.

"I didn't send you on a mission to marry Prince Thanos. I sent you to gain the royals' trust," he said, his eyes burning with hatred.

"I refused to marry Prince Thanos, but the queen pushed it through anyway!" Ceres said.

147

"What made the prince think he could marry you in the first place? Were you encouraging him?"

The crowd went silent, waiting for her answer.

"Can we please go somewhere quiet to talk," Ceres asked.

"No. I want everyone to witness this."

"Rexus, you know me. You have known me for years! Why are you doing this?" she asked.

"There must have been some reason he thought he should ask you."

"What? Rexus, I denied him!" Ceres yelled.

"Of all the people to betray me, I never thought you would."

"But I—" Ceres started.

"One of the princesses at the palace sought me out and told me she had seen you and Thanos in the library gardens, kissing," Rexus said.

"Stephania?" Ceres asked.

Rexus's eyes flared just a tad, then softened, and she hoped maybe he would finally listen.

"So it is not true?" he asked, a look of slight relief on his face.

"Stephania was supposed to marry Thanos, but when the king and queen saw their opportunity to create peace in the Empire, they broke off their engagement and—"

"First, answer my question. Did you kiss him?" he pressed.

She couldn't lie to him, but she could explain. Or at least try to.

"Yes. But—"

"And was it of your own free will and choice?" he continued.

She couldn't respond to that. She just couldn't, for so many reasons.

Rexus nodded, knowingly, his nostrils flaring, his expression hard again.

"So how can I then believe that you declined his proposal of marriage? Maybe you have even been sent as a spy here?" he said.

"No!"

"Get her out of here. And let it be known to every revolutionary that Ceres is banned from joining the rebellion forever!" Rexus said.

He swiveled around, but then stopped and glanced back at Ceres one more time, his expression disturbed.

"And I thought you should know. Nesos endured to the end. He gave his life for the rebellion while his sister was off flirting with the enemy."

She collapsed to the ground, her grief crushing her heart so thoroughly, she couldn't breathe, she couldn't see, her eyes overflowing with tears.

As the revolutionaries dragged her out of the cave, she called her brother's name again and again. Everything she had was now lost to her.

CHAPTER TWENTY SEVEN

"May I have a word?" Thanos asked Cosmas in the library, his hands shaking like leaves caught in a storm.

Cosmas looked up from reading a scroll, his expression worried, but loving.

"Of course."

They walked together out into the palace gardens and sat on a bench in front of the marble fountain, beneath a cloudy sky.

"What can I help you with, son?" Cosmas asked.

Thanos huffed.

"The king and queen commanded Ceres and I to be wed to restore the peace in the land," he said.

"So I heard."

"She rejected me."

"Ah, that, too, I heard."

Thanos took a deep cleansing breath.

"I have fallen in love with Ceres, but she believes I only proposed because I was commanded to."

Cosmas nodded, paused, and brought a hand to his chin.

"Have you spoken to her, opened your heart and let her know how you feel?" Cosmas asked."

"I told her some things, but I didn't tell her I loved her," Thanos relied.

"Heavens, why not?"

She had been so angry with him, he remembered, but that hadn't been why he had held back.

"When I was on my mission, I fought with her brother and he fell onto his sword and died. I told Ceres what happened, but she was so furious with me, it was as if she believed I had killed him."

Cosmas nodded, pondering.

"You told her the truth, and she will be devastated and angry and hurt for a time. If you had remained silent, and she found out, she would never have forgiven you. You did the right thing."

"But she hates me now, even though I tried to save her brother," Thanos said.

"I have known you your entire life, Thanos. You are a good man."

Thanos moaned.

"How am I a good man when I am ready to run away and leave everything behind?"

"Running away might offer you a new start, but soon the ghosts of the past will come to haunt you," Cosmas said. "You must talk to her, and then she can decide."

"She will not speak to me." Then Thanos had a thought. "Will you try and talk some sense into her?" he pleaded.

Cosmas bushy eyebrows grew heavy and he huffed.

"Very well, but only if you promise me you will tell her you love her."

Thanos nodded. "I promise."

*

Ceres ran back through the palace, dashing up the stairs three at a time. She tore past Empire soldiers who tried to arrest her, and darted toward Thanos's chamber, her feet moving so fast they barely touched the marble floors. Thanos was the only one who could help her at this point, she knew, and if he refused, she would drag him back to Harbor Cave bound and gagged if needed. Thanos needed to tell Rexus that she indeed had declined his proposal, and to allow her a chance to join the revolutionaries.

When she stormed into Thanos's room, she was sorely disappointed to find it empty.

She sprinted toward the palace gardens, looked in the royal practice arena, and even checked the blacksmith's chalet. But he was nowhere. It was as if Thanos had vanished into thin air.

The library, of course! she thought.

As she shot back through the gardens, she saw the queen standing on the veranda, eyes like a hawk, a hint of a conniving smile on her lips. And then four Empire soldiers rushed out from behind bushes and trees, arresting Ceres, their grips around her arms so tight it was painful.

"Thanos!" she screamed, thrashing legs. "Thanos!"

But he did not come.

The Empire soldiers dragged her upstairs to the queen's chamber, and threw her onto the shiny marble floor at the queen's feet. Two stood in front of the door, blocking it, while the other two marched past the stone statue of a couple embracing, and out onto the balcony, through the open doors.

"Come with me," the queen said to Ceres.

The queen walked out through the flowing purple curtains onto the veranda, overlooking the ocean. Shaken, but still angered, Ceres climbed to her feet and followed after.

"I still don't know how you managed to get out of your room," the queen said, her steely eyes gazing into the distance, a golden wine goblet in her hand. "At first, I thought you found a way to climb out the window and down the side of the tower, but there would be no way to do that and not fall to your death."

Ceres pinched her lips, not willing to offer up that Anka had freed her.

"So someone in the palace must have opened the door for you, and when I find out who that person is, I will personally skin them alive," the queen said, her voice flat but strict.

"It's not that difficult to unlock the door from the inside," Ceres said, hoping the queen would believe she did it on her own.

The queen glanced at Ceres, squinting.

"I doubt that is what you did," she said.

The queen turned away and peered across the ocean.

"When I was your age, I thought I could do whatever I wanted, too. Youth has a way of making one naïve and irrational," she said.

"I am neither of those things," Ceres said.

The queen took a sip of wine.

"Of course, you are, my dear. Your returning to the palace proves it. You should have stayed far away, Ceres. Here, we have your entire life planned out, and it will not be to your liking."

"I won't marry Thanos, if that's what you mean," Ceres said.

"You will, and as the new princess, it will be your responsibility to produce babies. Lots and lots of babies. You will never be seen. You will never be heard. Your children will not know you, for the instant they are out of your womb, they will be ripped from your arms to be raised by a nanny, far, far away."

"I won't marry Thanos."

"You have no choice, Ceres. You *will* wed him and once you have produced enough children, you will be killed off and replaced by another girl, a woman of royal blood, someone deserving of the title *princess*."

"Thanos would never let that happen. He's not like the rest of you barbarians."

The queen chuckled.

"Do you really think he cares for you?" she said, tsking. "Oh my. You are even more naïve than I thought."

Ceres's shoulders grew tighter with the queen's words. Had he only pretended to hate his family and the royals to gain her sympathy? Had he shown affection to try and make her fall for him when in truth, he didn't care for her at all? No, she didn't believe it. His touch and his kiss had been too real.

152

"Thanos told me a secret, and I must say, he is even more of a barbarian than the rest of us," the queen said.

"I doubt that," Ceres said, her guard up.

"I suppose he didn't tell you he was the one who sought out and killed your brother, Nesos?" the queen said, a glib smile on her lips.

With all her might, Ceres tried to keep her face free from expressing the pang of grief she felt on the inside, tried to force her eyes not to fill with tears. But she could not hold it all inside and fell onto hands and knees as racking sobs tumbled from her lips.

"Why...why are you doing this to me?" Ceres asked, her voice cracking. "How can you hate me so much when you don't even know me?"

The queen walked toward Ceres, stepping on Ceres's filthy dress.

"I don't need to know you to realize that you are a very useful pawn to the Empire," she said.

"I will never be your or anyone else's pawn," Ceres seethed.

The queen ignored her comment.

"Because of this marriage, peace will prevail through the land, allowing the Empire to maintain power. And when you have fulfilled your purpose, make no mistake, you will be discarded."

The queen nodded toward the Empire soldiers behind her, and they grabbed Ceres's arms and pulled her to her feet.

"Take her back to her room," the queen said. "And make sure both her wrists and ankles are shackled this time."

CHAPTER TWENTY EIGHT

Thanos always felt better after talking to Cosmas, and as he eagerly walked toward Ceres's chamber, he knew with every fiber of his being that the right thing was to open up to her, even if it meant she would not have him.

He marched through the palace gardens, and just as he came around the gazebo, he saw the king approaching with his advisors. His uncle must surely be the most evil man to roam the earth, Thanos thought, a cruel murderer who would go to any length to maintain his power over his subjects.

Thanos veered from the path, taking a different route, hoping the king hadn't seen him.

"Good day, Thanos," the king yelled, waving for him to come.

Thanos's skin crawled, but he approached his uncle as the advisors continued on down the path.

"Walk with me," the king said.

He strolled down the pathway beside his uncle and toward the royal practice ground, the scent of the flowers so sweet, it was nauseating. Or was it his uncle's presence that made him feel that way?

"I heard the proposal did not go as expected," the king said, hands clasped behind his back.

Of all the people in the world, the king was the absolute last person Thanos wanted to have this conversation with. But here he was, trapped, and with no choice other than to answer his uncle's prying questions.

"Not exactly," Thanos said.

The king was silent for a moment, perhaps waiting for Thanos to say something.

"I can see you care for this girl," the king finally said. "And it might surprise you to know that our stories are rather similar."

That did surprise Thanos, and his curiosity was piqued.

"When I first met Athena, she could hardly stand to be in the same room as me," the king said with a chuckle. "It was a blind marriage, one my parents had arranged in order to expand the Empire's borders. I had heard rumors of Athena's beauty and I could hardly wait to meet her, but when we met, Athena refused to acknowledge my existence in the least."

"Why?" Thanos asked, having never heard this story before.

"You see, she had fallen in love with someone else."

It was an interesting story, Thanos thought, but he failed to see how their situations were similar.

"We married, and after the first year, we became best friends, and passionate lovers," the king continued with a proud expression on his face.

"Why are you telling me this?"

The king paused, placing a fat hand on Thanos's shoulder.

"I realize our situations are not exactly the same, but I know you, Thanos. You will probably refuse to marry Ceres if she is not in agreement. And because she loves someone else, you will do everything in your power to not force her to marry you."

Thanos squinted.

"Why would you think she loves someone else?" he asked.

"We had Ceres followed when she snuck out of the palace to go visit Rexus, one of the leaders of the rebellion, and Ceres's lover," the king said.

If his uncle's words were true, it would indeed be another blow to Thanos's pride, but could he trust what his uncle was saying? Never.

"Rexus is her childhood friend, nothing more," Thanos said.

"I do not tell you this to be cruel. I tell you this so you will know the truth and not be deceived. I might be harsh on you, but I am always truthful," the king said.

Thanos slapped the king's hand away from his shoulder and took a step back.

"You lie," he snarled.

"When Ceres returned to the palace, she admitted everything to the queen. Ask Ceres yourself if you don't trust my word or the queen's," the king said.

Thanos shook his head in disbelief, but if the king were lying, why would he suggest Thanos ask Ceres in person?

He glanced up at the tower. Had he been blind? Did Ceres not return his affection? All the signs pointed to it: her snide comments, the way she maintained her distance from him, her refusal to marry him. Perhaps he had been mistaken, and now he paid the consequences: humiliation and rejection.

A surge of anger filled his chest, and he felt heat spread through his cheeks.

"In truth, Stephania is a much better match for you, Thanos. Ah, she might be a bit spoiled and full of herself, but motherhood will remedy all that."

"I don't love her," Thanos said through clenched teeth.

"I will allow you to make this decision yourself, Thanos. But know this: if you marry Ceres, it will ensure peace in the Empire and thousands of lives will be spared. If you do not, many will die on either side."

"If I agree to wed Ceres, the rebellion might die down for some time, but I can assure you they will rise again. I don't doubt you know that," Thanos said.

"Temporary or not, it would give us time to bring in additional forces from the north."

Thanos thought for a moment, but he knew he couldn't— wouldn't—marry someone who didn't love him in return.

"Think on it for a while," the king said. "In the meantime, General Draco has requested you lead a legion of men to quell the rebellion in Haylon."

At any other time, Thanos would have rejected the command without a second thought. His uncle was indeed shrewd as a serpent, he knew, offering him this opportunity now that Thanos was heartbroken. And he hated that he had been played yet again.

"When would I leave?" Thanos asked.

"Now. The ships stand ready in the harbor and the Empire soldiers are awaiting their new leader."

Thanos felt a wave of rage.

"I do not accept the position," he said.

The king smiled.

"You have no choice."

Thanos scowled.

"Then give me a chance, at least, to see Ceres before I go," he said, desperate to see her one last time, to explain to her that he might never return.

But the king merely shook his head.

"I am afraid that is impossible," he said.

And with those words, he walked away.

Thanos wanted to run to Ceres, but before he could move, a dozen soldiers surrounded him. He knew it would be no use. They would, upon the King's command, escort him to the ship, away from all of this, and to a battle that may mean his death.

CHAPTER TWENTY NINE

Sitting on a chair by the window in her chamber, her wrists and ankles chained, Ceres finally gave up trying to escape. For hours, she had strained to get out of these shackles, to summon the supernatural strength that sometimes granted her extreme power, but she was left with nothing but bruised flesh and bloodied skin.

Unsettled, trying to hold onto the dwindling sliver of sanity she had left, she gazed out the window at the serene capital. However, seeing how peace had descended over the war-torn city was of little help for nothing but deceit had brought this peace, she knew. How many more lies were out there floating around, keeping the infrastructure of the Empire from crashing down?

Ceres heard keys clatter outside the door, and when the door opened, to her surprise, in walked Cosmas.

He froze in the doorway, gasping when he saw her, a look of horror on his wrinkled face.

"Ceres, what happened to you?" he asked, immediately making his way over to her.

"The queen felt the need to confine me to my chamber," she said.

Cosmas examined the shackles, and when he saw her blood, he walked over to the water vessel, dipped a washcloth in it, and returned to her side.

"What a despicable thing to do to a sweet dear," he said, dabbing the washcloth on her sores. "Did she say why?"

Ceres bit down, the washcloth stinging as he cleaned her wounds.

"I refused to marry Thanos and then I left the castle," she said.

Cosmas paused, his expression saddened.

"Yes, he came to me, distraught, heartbroken," he said.

She blinked, trying to keep her tears at bay.

"I never wanted to hurt Thanos," she said. "But I refuse to have the Empire use us for their own gain."

Cosmas nodded, his brows knitting together.

"The queen said that I will only be used to breed babies and then I will be killed once I am no longer of use," Ceres said.

"I hope you know Thanos would never allow that," Cosmas said, continuing to clean her wounds.

"I didn't think he would. But now I don't know anymore."

Cosmas looked at her, his crinkly eyes a question.

"The queen said Thanos sought my brother out to kill him," Ceres said, a lump forming in her throat.

Cosmas gently placed a hand on her head, stroking her hair.

"My deepest condolences for your loss," he said. "Thanos told me what happened, and he was extremely distraught. He didn't know until after he had slain the young man that he was your brother. And he did all in his power not to slay him, even though Nesos tried to kill Thanos. Your brother fell on his own sword. A tragic misunderstanding, I am afraid. I am sure that if Nesos had known then he would not have tried to kill Thanos. But for Thanos's part, there was nothing more he could have possibly done. Nesos tried with all his heart to kill him. It was only his love for you that allowed Thanos to not fight back against a man who wanted his life."

So it wasn't as the queen said, Ceres noted with relief. The news made the loss slightly less horrific, although she still felt as if her heart might burst from sadness at any moment. But now she wondered, how many more of the queen's words were spiked with lies?

Cosmas looked Ceres in the eyes with such sincerity that she found herself holding her breath.

"Thanos loves you, Ceres. He needs a good, upright woman in his life to fight for him, with him, and to be on his side. Don't let the king and queen meddle in your relationship. Don't let them destroy what beauty is between you."

"Beauty? What beauty? He hasn't even had the decency to visit me," she said, a bitter taste in her mouth.

"He was sent on a mission to Haylon. The isle overthrew the Empire, and he was sent to get it back."

"What?" she asked in horror.

"Don't believe Thanos did it because he supports anything the Empire stands for," Cosmas said. "He most certainly does not."

He stepped closer and lowered his voice, and Ceres could sense he was going to say something dangerous, the air around them becoming tense.

"I overheard something," Cosmas said. "Thanos was told lies about you, and that is why he left for Haylon, despairing. It seems someone is trying to dispatch him and wants him dead. But I am not certain who or why."

"Who could possibly want Thanos dead?" she asked, worried.

"I know not. But whisper a word of this to anyone, and all of our lives will be in danger."

He took a step back, the atmosphere in the room returning to normal.

"There must be some way to get you out of the shackles. If only I had a key," he said, glancing around. "I'd sneak you out of here and bring you to my wife. You could stay with us in our home."

"You would do that for me?" she asked, realizing he'd be risking his life.

Cosmas smiled softly, his eyes brimming with tenderness.

"Thanos is like a son to me, and he loves you. I would do anything for him, and now you, too."

That brought tears to her eyes, Ceres having felt so alone and abandoned.

"Thank you," she said.

"I will be your faithful friend forever," Cosmas said. "You don't belong here, Ceres. Thanos cares for you, but the rest of the lot are rotten and vile, and you are too innocent and good to play their games."

Then she had a thought.

"If I write a letter to Thanos, is there any way you could deliver it for me?" she asked.

"Of course. I have a few friends, and I believe they could get it to Thanos rather quickly."

She pulled out parchment and started to write. She told him about everything, from what the queen had said, to why she had rejected his marriage proposal. She even told him that she did care for Rexus, but that she was confused because she loved them both. She told him about how she knew that the king and queen were pitting them against each other, but she had no way to prove it. She told him she had learned that he had killed her brother, but knew he hadn't intended it, and that she was trying to forgive him.

And finally, she asked him to return so she could hold him, keep him close, and she asked for his forgiveness for having been so cold.

She rolled the letter up and handed it to Cosmas.

"I will make sure this gets to Thanos, and I will protect it with my life if I have to," he said.

He embraced her, and then he left, locking the door behind him.

As Ceres listened to his footsteps vanish down the stairs, she couldn't help but wonder if she had been wrong about everything. If Thanos would get her letter. If he would be killed.

And if she would ever see Thanos again.

CHAPTER THIRTY

Ceres felt like her heart might leap out of her chest when she saw her father standing in the doorway of her chamber. He was dressed in fine clothing and his face was no longer pallid like it used to be, his cheeks rosy, his lips tilting upward. And those eyes… How wonderful it was to see his kind, loving eyes again, the eyes she trusted and immediately soothed her frazzled nerves.

She rose to her feet to run over to him, but the shackles restrained her.

His gaze fell upon the chains, and his expression turned worried. He strode across the chamber and reached arms around her.

She squeezed him tightly, nestling her face in his chest, the warmth of his body, the tenderness of his embrace, bringing tears of joy to her eyes.

"I missed you so," she whispered.

"I love you," he said.

For one blissful moment, they held each other, and all was beautiful and Ceres felt safe and loved.

But then she felt her father shrinking in her arms, vanishing little by little, his body imploding into nothingness, and it was as if she was herself dying with his departure.

"No," she whimpered as she grasped at him, trying to make it so he wouldn't disappear.

"Father!" she cried, closing her eyes, but then he was gone.

Sunlight warmed her face and she opened her eyes to find herself standing in the arena at the Stade, seven combatlords moving in on her, the crowd chanting for her blood to be spilt. Her hands and wrists were no longer shackled, but she had no weapons to defend herself with. Petrified, she searched her surroundings for a way to escape, but seeing the combatlords encircling her, there was no way out. Weaponless, she was incapable of fighting back, and when the combatlords charged toward her, she fell to her knees, shrieking, pressing the palms of her hands to her eyes.

Ceres woke up with a scream beneath the window, her body sweating, tears in her eyes, the stone floor cold and hard beneath her. The chains clattered when she buried her face in her hands, and she let out a piercing cry into the night.

What a horrid nightmare, she thought. But what did it mean? Was it an omen of what was to come? She hugged her chest, feeling so empty, so defenseless, so raw.

She startled when the door creaked open, and for a second, when she saw a male figure standing in the darkened doorway, in her half-awakened state she thought Thanos had returned.

"Thanos?" she whispered, excitement growing in her bosom.

"Is that what he does at night, visits you?" the man said.

The hairs on the back of Ceres's neck rose when she recognized the voice as Lucious's, and immediately she knew she was in danger, unable to escape, her wrists and ankles shackled.

"I hadn't seen you in a while and was worried about you," Lucious said.

"I doubt that."

He stepped closer, and his face appeared in the moonlight.

"Leave or I will scream," Ceres said, her breathing shallow.

"And who will come and save you? Not Thanos. Not the king of queen. Not Empire soldiers."

She rose to her feet and picked up a golden goblet from the table, throwing it at him, but he veered quickly, and the cup flew out the open door and tumbled down the steps.

Lucious slammed the door shut and lunged toward Ceres, pushing her wrists into the wall behind her, rubbing his body against hers, his breath reeking of alcohol.

She screamed and kicked him in the shin, but he clasped a hand over her mouth and pressed his knees between her legs so she couldn't move them. With hasty fingers, he pulled her skirt up, and for a moment, he released her mouth and crushed her lips with his.

Bile rose in her throat, and Ceres opened her mouth, biting him as hard as she could. He pulled back and hit her across the face, fist closed, his golden ring cutting Ceres across the cheek.

She forced herself to ignore the pain and screamed as loudly as she could, but he stuffed fabric down her throat, gagging her. His hands fumbled at her skirt again, and he pressed against her with forceful hips, a wild look in his eyes, the feral gleam of a savage.

"You have given me so much trouble that you owe me a little pleasure," he hissed.

Muffled sounds escaped her lips as she fought against him with all her might, but he was too strong and she was shackled.

Suddenly, he fell to the floor behind her, lifeless. She glanced over her shoulder and was flooded with relief to see Anka standing there with a silver candleholder.

"Anka," Ceres croaked, her knees trembling so she could barely stand.

Anka ran over to Ceres and hurriedly inserted a key into the cuffs around Ceres's ankles and wrists, freeing her.

Hands shaking uncontrollably, Ceres pulled the fabric out of her parched mouth. Anka grabbed Ceres's shoulders and looked her in the eyes.

"Soldiers are coming. Run!" Anka said.

"You have to come with me this time," Ceres said.

"No, I need to stay."

Anka spun around in a flash, dashed out the door, and disappeared down the dark stairwell, her rushed footsteps gradually vanishing.

Quickly, Ceres gathered her senses, forcing herself to move even though all she felt like doing was curling up into a ball in the corner and crying. On her way out the door, she gave Lucious a swift kick in the abdomen. She had despised him before, but now her hatred would burn every time she would see him. She would remember this moment, oh, how she would remember.

With sweaty hands, she stole down the stairwell, but just as reached the bottom, a slew of Empire soldiers approached her from the right, their swords drawn.

She looked to the left, but just as many Empire soldiers were storming toward her from that direction.

Then she heard footsteps behind her, but before she could turn around, she felt a hard object hit the back of her head, and everything went black.

CHAPTER THIRTY ONE

Stephania sat way in the back in the throne room and brought the fan to her lips, hiding a yawn, this dreary council of old birdbrained men and women so uninspiring she thought she might pass out from boredom. For hours, they had discussed—in that same mind-numbing monotonous tone—how the council was losing money, how the court was poorly managed, and how the rebellion, if it were to continue, would cost the Empire greatly. And as if these dignitaries couldn't grasp it, it had already been brought up *three* times that the rebellion had already drained half the king's gold.

Still, after hours of futile rambling, dozens of preposterous ideas being tossed around, they came up with no solutions. None. Stephania had sat through too many of these, and more and more, listening to these simpleminded mumbling nitwits, it just proved to her again that they were all brainless monkeys, pretending to know what they were talking about and what they were doing.

"Are there any more matters to discuss?" the king said from his throne at the front of the room.

Not a soul breathed a word, thank heavens, Stephania thought, dying to get out of this stuffy room, her bottom sore from having sat so long on this unpadded chair. Ever since the announcement that Thanos would wed Ceres, she had been demoted to sit in the back row by the exit door, next to the least important dignitary in the entire Empire, her seat the farthest from the king than anyone's.

I will climb my way back up into the king's graces, she resolved. Soon.

Just when she judged the meeting over, Cosmas, sitting at the front, rose and asked to stand before the king.

Stephania rolled her eyes. Would this day never end? She knew he was the old, senile, hard-of-hearing geriatric who cared about Thanos—a little too much, Stephania thought—but what on earth would he have to say that would warrant a single second in a council meeting such as this? All the old man did day in and day out was read scrolls in the library, stare at the stars, and talk of things that didn't really matter—not to the Empire at least.

Stephania noticed that the other dignitaries also seemed as disinterested in the old fart as her, their eyes glazing over with boredom.

Eying the floral pattern on her green silk dress, she listened with one ear, fanning herself as the ancient scholar held up a scroll toward the king.

"I was asked to deliver this letter to Thanos," Cosmas said. "It is from Ceres."

Stephania's ears perked right up. Perhaps the old scholar wasn't as much of a fool as she had thought. He had certainly misled me, Stephania thought, because she presumed the elder was more loyal to Thanos than even the king or the Empire. But perhaps she had been wrong in her assumption.

With a giddy heart, she repressed a smile. Now that commoner, Ceres, would be put to death and Stephania would marry Thanos, making everything right again. What fortune. What luck! Perhaps the gods were smiling down on her after all.

Stephania watched as the king read the letter in silence, his eyebrows sinking deeper and deeper over his fat face. When he had finished, he looked up.

"Did you read this?" the king asked Cosmas.

Cosmas stepped forward.

"Yes, and that was when I knew it needed to be brought to your attention," he said. "The girl is a lying conniving thief, a revolutionary in our very midst."

Gasps went through the chamber, and disorder erupted.

"Silence! Silence!" the king said.

"She must not marry Prince Thanos!" one advisor shouted.

"Hang the girl for treason!" another said.

The room exploded into commotion, some yelling for the king to imprison the imposter, others demanding she be put to death immediately.

"Silence!" the king yelled again, and the room settled down into a low hum of whispers. "We cannot just kill her. The revolutionaries will start rioting in the streets again and we are not ready to take upon all of them."

"But we must do something," an advisor said. "You do not mean to let a conspirator remain in our midst, leaking information to the revolutionary headquarters?"

A brilliant idea popped into Stephania's mind, and she gasped. A few heads turned toward her, and she smiled, knowing this idea would be her big chance to gain favor again. She just had to speak up.

"May I make a suggestion, Your Excellences?" she said loud and clear, rising to her feet.

The king's and queen's eyes darted to her.

"Please, it will also help to generate money for the Empire," she said, sensing their hesitation.

"Very well, speak," the king said. "But make it quick."

Stephania stepped onto the floor and walked toward the front of the room, her heels clicking against the marble floor, hundreds of eyes following her every step. She repressed a grin, bathing in the attention, elated that she had such a wonderful idea to present, when the supposed most powerful and intelligent men and women of the Empire had thought of no such thing. She knew that once she had shared with the king her idea, he would love it. And perhaps the king and queen would even give her more authority from now on—authority over Ceres.

Arriving at the bottom of the steps below the thrones, Stephania curtsied deeply before the king and queen.

"So far your excellences have done a wonderful job in using Ceres to promote and strengthen the Empire. And I see an opportunity to do it again," Stephania said.

"Well then, why don't you enlighten us," the queen said in a stiff tone.

"Don't throw Ceres out of our midst," Stephania said. "And don't execute her. Instead…use her to make the Empire wealthier than it has ever been."

The room grew silent, a few whispers throughout, and Stephania could just feel favor descending upon her again.

"And how do you propose we do that?" the king asked.

"Make her a permanent contender in the Killings," Stephania said.

Now the room had become so silent, Stephania could hear air moving in and out of her nostrils.

"She's a girl," someone yelled.

"No one would come see a commoner being butchered," another said.

Stephania was becoming impatient with these narrow-minded, short-sighted old-timers.

"Ceres is a soon-to-be royal female, a novelty, a fierce fighter in her own right," she said. "I have watched her fight, and she beat Lucious. I dare say people would travel from afar just to see her."

The king squinted, bringing a hand to his bearded chin.

"Make the spectators pay a premium to see the princess combatlord," Stephania added.

The king glanced at the queen, and the queen lifted an eyebrow.

"The princess combatlord," the king said. "I will think on it, but I do believe the idea to be excellent. Well done, Stephania. Well done."

Stephania curtsied again and walked back to her seat, extremely proud of herself for having thought of such a genius plan. Not only would her idea bring in money for the Empire, it would serve a very personal purpose, too.

Vengeance.

Finally, Thanos would be hers.

CHAPTER THIRTY TWO

What a waste of my time, Sartes thought as he sat below the willow tree in their yard, peeling potatoes for his mother, the wind pulling at his burgundy tunic in a steady stream. Sartes was too young to fight in the rebellion, Rexus had told him, and had sent him back home to sit and wait to mature, to feel useless, to ponder on Nesos's death, to sit and think of how Ceres was trapped within the walls of the palace, being abused, used, and tortured.

He tossed the potato into the pot and started to peel another one.

How was it Rexus expected him to sit here and do nothing, to suffer the consequences of the war, but to not help in any way? He wasn't too young, he knew, but the revolutionaries didn't see that. Just because he was small of build didn't mean he didn't have skills and abilities that were useful in the war against the Empire.

But no matter how much he insisted to Rexus on staying, Sartes was sent home to be with his mother to peel vegetables and wait on her hand and foot.

When he heard wheels crunching against the gravel road, Sartes looked up. The Empire's blue and gold banner waved above an enclosed wagon, dozens of Empire soldiers marching behind it in two perfectly straight rows.

The front door to the house creaked open, and Sartes's mother stepped out onto the front porch, squinting toward the cart, a hand shading her eyes, a generous frown on her face.

"Get inside the house, Sartes," she said.

"Mother—"

"Get inside the house now!" she screamed.

Sartes huffed and threw the knife into the bucket of water and potatoes. Heading toward the house, he fumed about how unfair it was that everyone treated him like a helpless child.

"And don't come out until I tell you to, do you hear?" his mother snapped.

Sartes slammed the door shut behind him and sat by the kitchen table, peering out through the partially opened shutter, seeing the Empire wagon slow to a halt right in front of their yard.

An Empire soldier hopped down from the driver's seat and approached, a scroll carrying the Empire seal in his hand.

"We are here to recruit your firstborn son for the royal army," the Empire soldier said, holding the scroll toward Sartes's mother.

Sartes saw that his mother glanced down at the scroll, but did not accept it.

"Ceres is my daughter, and as you know, she is to be wed to Prince Thanos," she said.

Sartes stood up and tiptoed to the shutter, listening intently.

"It has been ruled by the king that we recruit *all* firstborn males," the Empire soldier said.

"My eldest son is dead," she said, a tremble in her voice.

"And what of your other sons?" the Empire soldier asked.

"How dare you ask that of me?" Sartes's mother said.

"The king has not excused you or your family from serving him or the Empire. So I ask of you again, have you any other sons?" the Empire soldier continued.

"Even if I did have other sons, which I do not, he would soon be the prince's brother-in-law, and the royal army would not have claim upon him."

The Empire soldier took a threatening step toward her, and Sartes thought that he might strike his mother. He almost stormed outside, but he knew if he did, he would have to deal with his mother later, or he would be recruited to the royal army, and neither one of those options sounded tempting in the least.

"Might I assume you are with the rebellion then?" the Empire soldier growled.

"Why in heaven's name would you assume such a thing?" Sartes's mother asked.

"Because you are resisting the king's commands."

"I am not with the rebellion," she said.

"Will you obey the king's orders, then?"

"I will and I do."

"Then step aside so I can search your house."

"You have no right to search my home," she snapped.

"I have orders to kill anyone who resists!" the soldier roared. "Now stand out of my way, wench!"

Sartes gasped, realizing if he didn't get away, the soldiers would seize him and he would be forced to fight for the royal army. He started toward the back room, but as he did, he bumped into a chair, causing it to tip over with a crash. Stumbling forward, he just made it into the back room when he heard the Empire soldier kicking the front door in.

But before Sartes could escape through the window, the Empire soldier was upon him. The brute clutched Sartes's arm, pulling him out into the main room again, but Sartes grabbed a chair and swung it at the soldier, hitting him in the head so blood oozed from his brow.

The soldier cried out and fell to the floor, releasing Sartes's arm, and Sartes dashed into the back room again.

He tore open the shutters and hopped out the window, his heart pounding like a wild beast against his sternum, nothing on his mind other than getting to the field. He passed the shack, the meadow so close, but then he heard his mother screaming.

Unable to continue on, he turned around, and to his horror, he saw the Empire soldier holding a dagger up to his mother's throat.

"Mother!" he yelled, horrified.

"Please don't kill me," his mother croaked. "Sartes, you wouldn't let your mother die, would you?"

For a split second Sartes was conflicted. If he went back, he would be forced to fight against his friends, against all he believed in, freedom, prosperity, fairness. He would kill those he loved. He would be compelled to destroy all he knew in his bones and blood was the truth. But if he kept running, the Empire soldiers might catch up with him still, and his mother would be dead.

He couldn't live with himself knowing he was the reason his mother's throat had been slit by the enemy.

As three Empire soldiers ran toward him, he lifted his hands in surrender, his gaze on his mother, the relief in her eyes as the dagger was removed from her throat somewhat comforting. But also bitter.

The soldiers forced Sartes to the ground, jerking his arms behind his back, binding his wrists with rope. They pulled him up and dragged him past his mother, her eyes filled with tears.

"Sartes," she cried. "My baby."

She started after him toward the wagon, her arms longingly reaching for him, fingers straining at his shirt.

A soldier hit her across the face and she fell to the parched grass with a yelp.

The soldiers threw Sartes into the cart with three other young men and locked the door.

"I will never forgive myself for this," his mother cried. "Never!"

The driver whipped the horses and the wagon moved forward with a sudden jerk. Sartes's mother staggered to her feet and clamped her hands around the bars, eyes filled with desperation.

"Come back to me, Sartes, promise me this!"

But Sartes looked away and would not promise his mother anything. Because of her, he knew, his life was over. Because of her, he would have to fight on the side of the war that killed Nesos, on the side that stole Ceres from him, and on the side that had torn his family apart.

CHAPTER THIRTY THREE

The wind tugged at Rexus's hair as he feverishly galloped toward the palace beneath a blanket of stars, Anka sitting behind him holding on for dear life. August and Crates rode after them, their horses heavily loaded with weapons and gear hidden beneath wool throws.

Rexus hadn't been able to sleep a wink since he found out Ceres was engaged to Prince Thanos, the thoughts of them together an inescapable torment. He had judged Ceres a liar and a traitor, and had never wanted to see her again. He had never even wanted to *think* of her again either, but every thought that had occupied his mind these past days and nights had only been of her.

However, after Anka had approached Rexus in Harbor Cave earlier, everything had changed. When she had informed him that Ceres was shackled in the tower and had nearly been raped the night before last, and that Ceres had refused to marry Prince Thanos, he had felt sick to his stomach. But when Anka had told him Ceres loved him—Rexus—and that Ceres spoke of no one other than him, Rexus's heart had stopped, and he had realized with great remorse that Ceres had been nothing but loyal to the rebellion. And to him. And he had been a fool.

He swore, the pain too much to contain on the inside. He had been so hard on Ceres, had turned her away when she had begged to join the rebellion. And here she was doing nothing but supporting the revolution, fulfilling her job. He vowed that as soon as he saw Ceres again, he would beg for her forgiveness. This was entirely his fault, that she had been imprisoned. His pride had gotten in the way. He should have listened to her when she came to Harbor Cave, but like always, he was too quick to judge and was too much of a hothead.

He glanced back, seeing his friends were still right behind him. He had considered bringing twice as many men, but he figured if he brought more than two strapping young revolutionaries, the group might cause suspicion amongst the Empire soldiers who patrolled the streets of Delos at night. If he brought fewer, they wouldn't be able to ward off any potential Empire soldiers guarding Ceres's tower and the rescue mission would be a failure.

August was a new friend, young, happy, and built like a combatlord. He had joined the rebellion a mere month ago, and had told Rexus that he left his father—an advisor to the king—because of the way his father mistreated their slaves. Crates was one of

August's father's slaves, and the night August left, August took him with him, making Crates a free man.

Crates was tall and lanky, but exceptional with the bow and arrow, and having lived in lack his entire life, he had a fire about him that Rexus loved, the young man embodying the spirit of the revolution.

Clouds had started to roll in when they reached the city, and as the night darkened, Rexus led them through the back streets in silence, passing crowded houses, some intact, others demolished by the Empire.

By the time they paused in an alleyway across from the palace, the heavens had cleared again, the moon and stars bringing welcome light.

Anka descended from the horse, and peeking out from behind the wall, she pointed out the tower Ceres was imprisoned in.

"I have to go back inside," Anka said. "If anyone finds out I have been gone…"

"Yes, go," Rexus said. "And Anka…"

Anka turned around and looked at him.

"Thank you," he said.

She nodded, and he watched as Anka vanished into the night down the street, around the stone wall toward the back entrance of the palace.

Rexus took a moment to study the Empire soldiers who marched around the wall, noting that they passed by approximately every five minutes. It should give them ample time to climb the wall and not get caught.

Hurriedly, they tied up the horses, took the weapons and rope, and just as the next Empire soldier marched by, seeing the coast was clear, Rexus led August and Crates toward the outer wall.

The wall was slick, but with ropes tossed over the wall, anchored in the trees on the other side, the climb took no time at all.

After they had descended the wall, making no sound as they hopped down onto the soft, green lawn, they stole toward the palace, hiding behind trees and bushes.

Once at the bottom of the tower, Rexus peered up the side of the rounded wall. The structure was higher than what he had initially thought, but he was confident he would be able to climb it and bring Ceres down with him once he had freed her. Any thought of slipping and falling he forced away, knowing uncertainty could cause him to fall.

"Wait behind the bushes while I get her," Rexus said to August and Crates. "If any Empire soldiers approach, warn me with a quail call."

He removed his cloak and handed it to August.

"Be safe," August whispered, vanishing into the shadows with Crates.

Rexus attached a rope to the end of his arrow and shot it through the partially opened shutter. He paused, looking up, hoping Ceres would come to the window, but he saw no movement.

He tugged on the rope, and seeing it was secure, he wedged his foot between two rocks and started the climb. One foot after another, pulling on the cord, he inched his way upward, his hands clamping, the muscles in his arms flexing, his feet digging into the niches of the stone wall.

Halfway up the tower there was a generous ledge, and Rexus paused to rest, panting heavily. He looked down and saw nothing but bushes and trees and shadows. August and Crates were certainly hiding well, he noted.

Once he had caught his breath, he continued to climb, and soon his heart was again pounding from exertion. Or was it from the thought of seeing Ceres?

He strained, climbing faster, just trying to reach her, to see her smile again, her beautiful eyes, feeling her soft skin.

A few inches from the top, he stopped, thinking he heard something below, but when he looked, he saw nothing.

Finally, he reached the ledge of her window and peered into the room.

"Ceres," he whispered.

"Rexus?" he heard Ceres speak, amazement in her voice.

Then he saw her face—a desperate expression—and that she wore a royal gown that was torn and filthy. When she gripped his hands, he felt how cold she was, but how strong she was, too. She pulled him inside.

"You came for me," she said, throwing her arms around him.

"I'm sorry for what I said," he said, gripping her tightly, never wanting to let go. "I love you, with all that I am."

"I love you, too," she said. "I'm sorry."

He pulled back and stroked her hair, gazing into her eyes. She rose up onto the balls of her feet and pulled at the back of his head so their lips met. He kissed her passionately, pouring all of himself, all the longing and regret, into that kiss. Her lips were soft, and he knew they were destined to be together.

They parted.

"We have to hurry," he said. "There will be time later."

She nodded.

He drew the dagger from its sheath around his waist so he could free her from the shackles.

Suddenly Rexus felt an excruciating pain in his back. He couldn't breathe.

He looked down and, to his horror, saw an arrow tip protruding from his chest, running all the way through his body.

Then, before he could register what was happening, there came another.

He was being attacked from behind, he realized. The guards below must have spotted him. He had been shot from behind.

Rexus reached out for Ceres, but his world was already darkening. Before he could sever her bonds, he found himself instead losing balance, falling backwards.

And then he tumbled out the window.

Rexus fell as if in slow motion, the wind in his ears, the sound of Ceres's scream following him, the air so thin and warm. There was no resistance. It seemed a long way down, as if he were sinking into the earth and the earth swallowed him whole. Would not the ground soon come?

The last thing he saw before he hit the ground was Ceres's contorted face, looking down, wishing, as he, that everything had turned out differently.

CHAPTER THIRTY FOUR

Thanos, standing at the bow of his ship, the scent of the ocean filling his nostrils, spotted Haylon in the distance, and immediately regret brewed in his chest. With every breath he had taken on this trip, every inch he had sailed, the regret had only grown stronger. Now, with the destination in plain sight, it suddenly became crystal clear: he knew he had made the wrong decision not to take Ceres from the castle and run from his uncle, from everything he knew.

And in this moment, his regret turned to shame. Yes, he felt ashamed for letting the king play him again, this time pitting Ceres and him against each other.

Waves crashed against the ship below, drops of salt water splashing onto his overheated face. A steady stream of brisk sea breeze ran through his hair as he watched the gulls dive into the sea only to rise from the ocean with fish in their beaks.

If only I were that free, he thought.

He still felt seasick, and had since the day the ship left the shores of Delos one week earlier to sail south. Now, seeing Haylon, it made him want to jump into the ocean, swim to shore, and worship the white sandy beaches surrounding the isle. Land, solid earth, he thought. He never realized he would miss it so much.

A sense of awe went through him as his eyes scanned the paradise in the near distance. The isle, a hub of trading between all western nations, was dramatically beautiful, he could see as they approached, with towering verdurous mountains behind the city, rising from the sea, the buildings glistening golden in the evening sunlight. It was his first time here, and the closer they sailed, the more he wished his first visit were under different circumstances completely—not to kill the inhabitants, or to destroy the beautiful architecture of their most magnificent buildings.

His eyes followed the snaking road that ran from the city entrance up past domes and towers, and all the way up to the castle, resting on a hill. That was the road General Draco had described in strategy meetings, the road they would travel to seize the castle. The road where blood would flow. The road that would be unrecognizable after they had marched through it. The wall around the city was tall, but with ladders, ropes, catapults, and flaming arrows, tens of thousands of Empire soldiers attacking at once, the city would be theirs soon enough, General Draco had said. And indeed it would, Thanos knew.

When he turned around to behold his crew, the tension on board had become so thick it felt like a wall around him. Was it more than just the nerves of the warriors he was detecting? The entire trip, Thanos had sensed someone or something watching him, although when he felt eyes burning at the back of his neck, he'd turn around to find no one and no thing. He would brush it off, thinking he was growing paranoid, but just when he had forgotten about it, again, it would suddenly be as if cold fingers were creeping down his spine.

He nodded toward General Draco, who stood by a giant of a man, wearing golden armor and a visored helmet. The hulk was the tallest Empire soldier Thanos had ever seen, a true giant. The Typhoon, the rest of the men on the ship called him, although Thanos doubted that was his real name. It was rumored the Typhoon had taken on a group of twenty wild northern warriors at once, and had killed them all in under five minutes.

General Draco and the Typhoon would lead the attack on the great city, and Thanos would bring in the second group of troops once the main gates had been opened. They would attack immediately, General Draco had ordered, not give the rebels of Haylon a chance to gather their armies, although Thanos didn't doubt they had already seen their fleet of ships and that their army was more than ready to defend the city. No one would be able to defend against the numbers King Claudius had sent, Thanos knew.

Hundreds of rowboats were lowered onto the choppy azure ocean, and the Empire soldiers descended into the vessels with weapons and heavy armor. Some larger boats carried catapults and boulders.

General Draco invited Thanos into his boat, and Thanos took a seat next to the Typhoon. He felt like a dwarf next to the beast.

"Remember, the goal is to take the city in under an hour, before nightfall," General Draco said. "Kill anyone who resists."

"We will spare the women and children, correct?" Thanos said.

"As long as they obey," General Draco said. "As long as they bow before the Empire's banner and pledge to submit to the king's laws."

"I don't see how the women and children will be a threat, even if they did resist," Thanos said.

"It is the king's orders. I do not question them," General Draco snapped, glaring at Thanos.

Thanos looked away, but he made a decision to not kill women or children—not even if they rebelled.

They arrived at shore and Thanos hopped out of the boat, the warm water reaching right above his knees as he hauled the heavy oak vessel toward land with other Empire soldiers. Just as he glanced back, Thanos noticed that General Draco and the Typhoon looked at each other, and then the general nodded before heading toward the white, sandy beach.

At first, Thanos considered the gesture somewhat suspicious, but when the general turned to him and nodded, too, he thought nothing more of it.

The boats were hauled ashore, the weapons and artillery placed into wagons, and the Empire soldiers organized into twelve battalions, Thanos to lead one of them.

He took his place in front of his men and led them southward, down the coastline, wading through ankle-high water. He felt that familiar sensation running through him, a combination of excitement, fear, and adrenaline: the battle was about to begin.

Yet Thanos had not gone very far, the water still splashing on his ankles, when suddenly, without warning, he felt a shooting pain in his upper back.

He dropped to his knees, stunned, not understanding what was happening.

He felt cold metal in his back, and with a start, he realized: he had been stabbed.

He knelt there, lightheaded, not understanding. They were still far off from reaching the enemy.

Then Thanos felt the sword being pulled out of him, and he shrieked, the pain unbearable. He looked up to see the Typhoon step in front of him, wiping the blade of his sword clean of Thanos's blood.

He grinned down, and that was when Thanos realized: he was being assassinated.

And no one was turning to help him.

"Any last words?" the Typhoon asked, his voice impossibly deep.

Thanos gasped for air.

"Who sent you?" he managed to ask.

"I will tell you," the Typhoon replied. "When you're dead."

CHAPTER THIRTY FIVE

Ceres sat in the dungeon on the damp floor, her back against the cold stone wall, fully defeated as an endless stream of tears trailed down her face. How—how was she to continue on? Thanos had left her. Nesos was dead. And worst of all, Rexus…

She let out a faint sob and inhaled a jagged breath as the memory came rushing back. Rexus, shot in the back, falling from her reach, backwards, out of the tower window. Torn away from her when they had been so close, so close to starting a new life together.

It was too cruel.

Ceres sobbed. There was nothing more to fear now, she realized. Not even her life mattered anymore, it seemed.

She did not know how much time had passed when she heard footsteps coming down the hallway. She didn't move. She was beyond caring what the royals did to her, so much so that if they were coming to kill her, she would welcome the merciful death.

A woman and three men appeared on the other side of the bars. Ceres refused to look up, but she knew from the overly sweet rose perfume that the woman was Stephania.

An Empire soldier unlocked the cell, but Ceres's gaze remained on the floor. She would not acknowledge them.

"You have been ordered to the Stade," an Empire soldier said.

Ceres didn't move.

"You will compete in the Killings."

Ceres felt the life rush out of her. So. They would kill her after all.

The soldier grabbed her by the arm, jerked her to a standing position, and bound her wrists behind her back. When Ceres finally looked up, she saw Stephania smiling.

Stephania stepped forward.

"Before you die," she said, venom in her voice, "I thought you might like to know something."

She leaned in close, her breath uncomfortably hot on Ceres's neck.

"I sent a messenger to Haylon," she said, "bearing a very special message. I told Thanos never to defy me. Never to make a fool of me. Now, finally, he has learned why."

She beamed, satisfied, though Ceres did not know why.

"Thanos," she said, "is dead."

*

The Empire soldiers hauled Ceres through the musty dungeon corridor and up the stairwell. They dragged Ceres outside and led her to an enclosed horse-pulled wagon. Once the door was locked and the soldiers had taken their seats at the front, the wagon rolled out of the palace courtyard and onto the streets of Delos. They passed houses, and weaved through hordes of citizens making their way to the Stade.

Ceres hardly took notice of her surroundings; everything passed by in a blur. Nothing mattered anymore. Everyone she loved was either far away or dead.

In a daze, she realized they were moving through Fountain Square, and Rexus's face flashed before her eyes. Just weeks ago they were here, happy, hopeful, free.

And just yesterday, he had been in her arms, professing his love; and a moment later, he had fallen to his death. How could a being so vibrant, so alive, now be nothing more than a memory?

Outside the Stade, the wagon creaked to a halt. An Empire soldier dragged her out of the cart and into the tunnels.

They marched past combatlords and weapon-keepers, the chants of the crowd reaching her all the way down here.

Finally, the soldier threw her into a small chamber and ordered her to change into the armor lying on the bench. He left, locking the door behind him.

Alone, Ceres undressed and slipped on the leather skirt and breastplate. They were studded with gold, and were soft and new, she could see, custom made for her, fitting perfectly. She pulled on the boots, noticing they were also her size, the leather supple, the ends of the laces embellished with gold.

All these years she had dreamt of becoming a combatlord, of wielding a sword in an arena in front of thousands of spectators.

And yet now, she hated being here. Somehow, the king and queen had stolen her dream, tarnished it, and had forced her to fight for the very people she despised.

Not a minute later, the Empire soldier returned and ordered her to follow.

They walked through the dim tunnel, past weapons, past dozens of fallen combatlords and their weapon-keepers. Arriving by the gate, Ceres heard the crowd roaring outside, and her stomach clenched tightly.

"Paulo will be your weapon-keeper," the Empire soldier said.

She turned to see Paulo, rather short in stature, nothing but a bundle of muscle with dark smooth skin. His black hair framed a heart-shaped face, and he had a few whiskers on his chin below full lips.

"It will be an honor to serve you," Paulo said with a nod, handing her a sword.

Ceres didn't want to reply. She didn't want this to be her reality.

"Ceres and Paulo are next!" an Empire soldier called.

Even though Ceres no longer feared for her life, her hands shook, as her throat dried up.

The iron gates opened with a rattle, and Ceres looked out into the arena and saw two Empire soldiers hauling a dead combatlord toward the tunnels.

Taking a deep breath, she stepped into the Stade.

The roar was deafening, the sunlight warm against her skin, the brightness stinging her eyes as she scanned the over-packed audience.

"Ceres! Ceres! Ceres!" they chanted.

As her eyes grew accustomed to the sunlight, she let her gaze wander across the arena. On the other side of the stadium stood a barbarian of a combatlord, his arms as thick as Ceres's waist, the veins in his legs bulging on top of thick, swollen muscles.

She clenched the hilt of her sword and knew that this man would kill her. She glanced at Paulo, and saw his face had fallen.

But she would not back down.

With all the courage she had inside of her, she raised her sword.

Her entire life she had been a slave. And now, even though she may very well die, that part of her life, she realized, was over.

Now, finally, she would go from Slave to Warrior.

Now, death would come for her.

And now her life would begin.

The crowd roared.

"CERES! CERES! CERES!"

COMING SOON!

Book #2 in Of Crowns and Glory

Books by Morgan Rice

THE WAY OF STEEL
ONLY THE WORTHY (BOOK #1)

VAMPIRE, FALLEN
BEFORE DAWN (BOOK #1)

OF CROWNS AND GLORY
SLAVE, WARRIOR, QUEEN (BOOK #1)

KINGS AND SORCERERS
RISE OF THE DRAGONS
RISE OF THE VALIANT
THE WEIGHT OF HONOR
A FORGE OF VALOR
A REALM OF SHADOWS
NIGHT OF THE BOLD

THE SORCERER'S RING
A QUEST OF HEROES
A MARCH OF KINGS
A FATE OF DRAGONS
A CRY OF HONOR
A VOW OF GLORY
A CHARGE OF VALOR
A RITE OF SWORDS
A GRANT OF ARMS
A SKY OF SPELLS
A SEA OF SHIELDS
A REIGN OF STEEL
A LAND OF FIRE
A RULE OF QUEENS
AN OATH OF BROTHERS
A DREAM OF MORTALS

THE SURVIVAL TRILOGY
ARENA ONE (Book #1)
ARENA TWO (Book #2)

the Vampire Journals
turned (book #1)
loved (book #2)
betrayed (book #3)
destined (book #4)
desired (book #5)